March 1, 1968, was the day Johnny Cash married June Carter. I wanted their marriage to work, but I didn't think it would. He was such a rebel, probably even did drugs, and everyone knew June was just a darling.

Nate called me the next day. I wasn't in a good frame of mind, missing him, and feeling so alone, since I no longer had either my family or the sisters to turn to.

I tried to explain my feelings to him but knew I'd failed miserably when he asked, "Are you having second thoughts?"

"No. Not at all." Surprisingly, I wasn't. "The one thing that seems to be a constant in my life is my certainty about marrying you."

"You're sure of that?"

"Absolutely."

"Because if you're having second thoughts, we need to talk about them, Eliza."

"I'm not!" I got cold then. "Nate, are you trying to tell me *you've* changed your mind?"

"No." His response was unequivocal. "I love you, Eliza."

"I love you, too."

Dear Reader,

Once in a lifetime a writer has a story like this one.
If she's lucky. It's the story of a great love. The story of
a woman. It's a story inspired by my mother and father,
based loosely on their marriage.

My mother was nineteen when she met my father. She'd
been raised in a Catholic family, attended Catholic school,
and after graduating, had visited with an order of nuns
called the Little Sisters of the Poor. My father was
thirty-two when they met. He'd been divorced three
times (twice from the same woman). He was playing
piano in a bar. And living two states and a Great Lake away.

Following a couple of weekend visits and many phone
calls, my father asked my mother to marry him two
months after they met. That same year, disowned by most
of her family–and some of his–and rejected by her church,
she did so.

I've heard the tale countless times, knowing there'd come
a time when I had to write it. What follows here is my
story–about two fictional people with fictional lives,
but the love and example they show as they make their
own choices reflect the same values and gifts I witnessed
between my parents.

This is the legacy they've left to me. And I pass it on to
you....

Tara Taylor Quinn

P.S. I love to hear from readers. You can reach me at
www.tarataylorquinn.com or P.O. Box 13584, Mesa,
AZ 85216.

The Night We Met

Tara Taylor Quinn

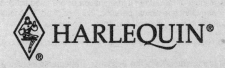

HARLEQUIN®

TORONTO • NEW YORK • LONDON
AMSTERDAM • PARIS • SYDNEY • HAMBURG
STOCKHOLM • ATHENS • TOKYO • MILAN • MADRID
PRAGUE • WARSAW • BUDAPEST • AUCKLAND

ISBN-13: 978-0-373-65408-6
ISBN-10:   0-373-65408-1

THE NIGHT WE MET

ABOUT THE AUTHOR

With more than forty novels, published in twenty languages, to her credit, Tara Taylor Quinn is a *USA TODAY* bestselling author. She is known for her deeply emotional and psychologically astute stories. Tara is a three-time finalist for the Romance Writers of America's RITA® Award, a multiple finalist for the National Readers' Choice Award, the Reviewers' Choice Award, the Booksellers' Best Award and the Holt Medallion. Tara also writes romantic-suspense fiction for MIRA Books. Her most recent MIRA title, *In Plain Sight,* was critically acclaimed and will be followed in October 2007 by *Behind Closed Doors.* When she's not writing or fulfilling speaking engagements, she enjoys traveling and spending time with her family (including several dogs!) and friends.

For Agnes Mary and Walter Wright Gumser—
together forever. Thank you.

Chapter 1

January, 1968
San Francisco, California

Life started the night we met. Everything before this was merely preparation for what was yet to come. It was a Saturday evening and I'd gone to a local pub just down the street from St. Catherine's Convent. I'd been living in a private dormitory at the convent for a couple of years, studying education at the small elite women's college a block away—and was just two weeks from becoming a St. Catherine's postulant and beginning my life of poverty, chastity and obedience. The San Francisco pub wasn't a place I frequented often, but that

January night I needed the noise, the distraction, as much as I wanted the beer that I would drink only until it got me past the unexpected tension I felt that night.

After all, I had prayers and then Mass with the sisters early the next morning, followed by religious study.

At a little table some distance from the shiny mahogany wood bar, I sipped my beer, watched merrymakers and pool-players, and contemplated the fact that I didn't belong anywhere.

Not on a date. Or at home watching television with my family. Not out with friends, not in a library studying and certainly not on the completely empty dance floor in front of me.

I was an in-between, having left behind the person my parents, siblings and friends, knew me to be. And yet I hadn't arrived at who I was going to become. The friends I'd known were getting married, having babies, exploring the world and its opportunities while I was living on the outskirts of a society I was on the verge of joining. I had three years of religious study ahead of me before I'd be allowed to take my final vows and become one of the sisters with whom I'd soon be living.

Don't get me wrong, I wasn't sitting there feeling sorry for myself. I'm far too practical and stubborn and determined to waste my time on such a defeatist emotion. I was simply taking my life into my own hands even as I gave it to God. Trying to understand the reasons for my decisions. Testing them. Making sure. Soul-searching, some folks might call it.

For that hour or two, I'd left my dormitory room at the convent and all that was now familiar to me, left the sisters and their gentle care, to enter a harsher world of sin and merriment and ordinary social living to seek the truth about me.

Was my choice to wed myself to God, to serve him for the rest of my days, the right one for me, Eliza Crowley, nineteen-year-old youngest child of James and Viola Crowley?

A woman's laugh distracted me from my thoughts. A young blond beauty settled at the recently vacated table next to me with a man good-looking enough to star in cigarette commercials. They held hands as they sat, leaning in to kiss each other, not once but twice. Open-mouthed kisses. The girl wasn't much older than me, but she had a diamond on her finger whose karat weight was probably triple that in my mother's thirtieth-anniversary band.

I couldn't imagine any of that for myself. Not the hand-holding. The kissing. And certainly not the diamond. They were all fine and good and valid for some lives. Just too far removed from me to seem real.

As I drank my beer, I saw an older woman sitting at the bar. I had no idea when she'd come in. The place was crowded, the seats at my table the only free ones on the floor, but I'd pretty much noticed everyone coming and going. Except for this woman.

Had she appeared from the back room? Was she working there? Maybe a cook? She held her cigarette with her left hand. There was no ring.

Judging by the wrinkles and spots on that hand, I figured she had to be at least sixty.

Had she always lived alone?

Could I?

I pictured the house I might have—a single woman by myself. It would be white with aluminum siding, and a picket fence and flowers. I was inside, having dinner, I thought. A salad, maybe. I'd worked that day. I'm not sure where, but I assumed I'd be a teacher. I was patient enough. And I liked kids.

And the whole vision felt as flat as the tile floor beneath my feet. There was nothing wrong with that life. It just wasn't mine.

I imagined being my sister, my mother. I loved them, admired them—and experienced no excitement, no sense of connection, when I considered their choices for myself. I pictured myself as Gloria Steinem. I had courage and determination. Perhaps there was some contribution I was supposed to make to the world, some discovery or mission.

But I didn't think so. There was no fire, no zeal at the thought. Rather than change the world, I felt compelled to care for those who lived in it.

What about that woman over there at the bar, surrounded by people yet talking to no one, lighting up another cigarette. Was there something I could do to help her? Comfort her?

I didn't know, but if she asked for help I'd give it. Regardless of any discomfort. I was here to serve.

I wanted to be God's servant, ready for Him to send where He needed, when He needed.

Joan of Arc wasn't my heroine. Mother Theresa was.

I'd made the right choice.

Satisfied, relaxed, I reveled in my quieted mind and a few minutes later I was ready to leave the half mug of beer on the table and head back to St. Catherine's. I planned to write about tonight in my journal, chronicling for later years these moments of reflection and self-revelation. I was mentally titling the page *The night I knew for sure.*

I just had to find the waitress so I could pay my bill. Good luck doing that, since the bar was so crowded. I couldn't even catch a glimpse of her. How much did a beer cost in this place? Surely fifty cents would do it, plus tip. I'd shoved a few bills in the front pocket of my blue jeans.

"Hey, don't I know you?"

I started to tell the blond guy standing at my table that the line was wasted on me, but then I recognized him.

"You're Patricia Ingalls's older brother, Arnold." My reply was pretty friendly to make up for thinking he was hitting on me.

"Right," he said, smiling. "And you're that friend of hers who decided to become a nun."

Not quite how I would've said it, but…okay. He was, after all, correct. "Yep."

"My friends and I just drove in from skiing at Tahoe—and this is the only table left with seats. Mind if we join you?"

I fully intended to tell him he could have the table. I

was leaving, anyway. And then I noticed the guy who'd joined the group, pocketing a set of keys. Arnold was older than Patricia and me by four years. This guy was even older.

It wasn't his age that froze my tongue, though. I'm not really sure *what* it was. He looked at me and I couldn't move.

And somehow, five minutes later, I found myself sitting at a table sipping beer with five athletic-looking older men.

And buzzing with nervousness because of the man right next to me—Nate Grady, Arnold had said, adding that Nate was staying sober so he could drive, which explained the keys.

Was I drawn toward him as a woman is to a man? I didn't think so. Not that I knew much about such things. It was just that he was so…vital.

I couldn't understand my reaction so, really, had no explanation for it.

"When'd you quit the convent?" Arnold asked after the beer had been served.

"I didn't." My eyes shied away from any contact with Nate as I replied—and my entire body suffused with guilty heat. For a second there, I'd wanted to deny my association with the church. With my calling.

Like Peter? Who later redeemed himself?

Or Judas—who never did?

"No kidding!" Nate's deep voice was distinctive, his words clear in the room's din. "You're a nun?"

He'd been a minute or two behind, parking the car, when Arnold had mentioned it earlier.

"Not yet," I assured him as though there was still time to stop the course of my life if need be—and at the same time shrinking inside, preparing to be struck down for my heresy.

"I've been living at St. Catherine's dormitory for the past couple of years, but in two weeks I move into the convent itself and start my formal training," I added to appease any anger I might have instilled in God, directing my comment to Nate without actually looking at him. "It takes three years to get through the novitiate."

"You live with the nuns?" That voice came again, touching me deep inside.

"I live in a dormitory on the grounds, yes."

"Dressed like that?"

"Not around the convent, no." I didn't describe the plain brown dress I usually wore. Not understanding why his presence was like a magnet to me, I wasn't going to engage in conversation with him at all if I could help it. I tried to focus on Arnold and the other guys as they relived, with exaggerated detail I was sure, antics from their day, each trying to top the other with tales of daring attempts or perilous danger survived.

But frankly, I found their accounts boring. I kept thinking about paying my bill and excusing myself. Our waitress passed, laden with drinks and I told myself I'd flag her down next time.

"Do you spend your days with the nuns?"

I shook my head, alternating between wishing I'd bothered with makeup or a hairstyle and feeling glad that I hadn't. Men liked blond bobs, not the straight brown wash-and-wear stuff that was cut just above my shoulders.

There was safety in mousy.

And in another six months when, God willing, I became a novice and received the Holy Habit, minus the wimple I'd be honored with when I took my final vows, my hair would be cut as short as my father's.

"What kind of order is St. Catherine's?"

Why wasn't he joining in the boasting with his friends?

"Teaching. Other than those who run the household, the sisters hold teaching positions, either at the private college I attend or at Eastside Catholic High School right next to it."

I didn't see how he could possibly be interested in this. And wasn't even sure he'd be able to hear me above the crowd.

"So that's what you want to do? Teach?"

"I want to serve God. Since the Second Vatican Council there's been a surge of energy directed toward education. And I love kids. So, yes, I do hope to spend my life teaching." Instinctively I turned to face him as I spoke. And couldn't look away. He had the bluest eyes I'd ever seen. And possibly the warmest.

"How old are you? If you don't mind me asking."

"Nineteen."

He leaned a bit closer, not disrespectfully, I somehow knew, but simply to ease conversation.

"Do you have any idea how lucky you are to know your calling in life at such a young age?"

The question reminded me of my reason for being in the pub at all—potentially the last time I'd enter such an establishment. "Yes," I told him, remembering the conclusions I'd drawn only a half hour before. And the resulting peace that had settled over me.

A peace I couldn't feel quite as intensely anymore...

"So what happens next week? Do you quit school?"

"No. I only have a few more classes to take before I get my degree and I can attend those during my postulant period. That's what I begin in two weeks."

"How's that different from what you're doing now?"

I could hear Arnold on my other side, delineating in great detail a downhill run he'd made that day.

"I'll be moving into the Mother House—the main house where the nuns live. Other than classes, I'll be pretty much restricted to living there. My day will start at 5:00 a.m. and end at 10:00 p.m. I'll have a uniform, mostly black, with a veil but no wimple, and my only possessions, besides my rosary and hygienic necessities, will be a sewing kit. Except for grace, meals will be taken in silence, and most general conversation will be limited to designated free time during the day. In another six months, when I become a novice, I'll read only religious books, and will have no access to radio, television or newspapers so that I can focus completely on prayer, meditation and spirituality."

He'd asked. But I think I answered as much for me

as for him. Hearing myself say the words out loud made them real. Official. I was prepared. And unafraid.

"And you're doing this because you want to?"

There was no derision or criticism in his tone—just honest curiosity that spoke to my heart. "I can't imagine doing anything else," I told him with a certainty born earlier that evening.

"What does your family think of it all?"

"I'm the youngest of five and my folks have been shaking their heads at me for as long as I can remember." I smiled. "Mostly they approve. They've already got sixteen grandchildren. And they're devout Catholics. They're proud that one of their offspring is dedicating her life to God's service."

"But you don't feel they're pressuring you to go through with it?"

"Not at all." That I knew for sure because we'd talked about it. Several times. "They want me to have a decent, productive life doing something that makes me happy."

"You're very lucky."

I almost didn't hear him. I considered letting that be the end of the strange conversation that had sprung up from nothing. But as I thought about what he'd said, I knew I couldn't just get up and leave.

"You don't think your parents want the same thing for you?" I couldn't believe I was asking such a personal question of a total stranger.

"Probably."

The response left a lot unsaid, but I wasn't forward enough to press further.

"What do you do?" I asked instead, with a genuine desire to know. Nate Grady, as a member of the human race, intrigued me.

"I manage a ski resort in Boulder, Colorado."

"What about in the summer?"

"We have camp activities for kids, hiking for adults."

"So how did you meet Arnold?"

"My kid brother and Arnold were part of a ski team training for the junior Olympics several years ago and stayed in touch. After high school, Keith enlisted, said it was the only way he'd ever get a degree. I offered to help him pay for college, but he wouldn't let me. His unit was deployed to Vietnam almost as soon as he got out of boot camp and two years ago, we got word that he'd been killed. A couple of weeks later, his remains were sent home for burial." He paused, and when he resumed speaking, his voice was slow and measured. "Arnold and I have this sort of unspoken agreement to fill some of the gaps left by Keith's loss, so we go skiing together a few times every year."

The words could have hung like lead between the strangers we were, but they didn't. Nate's openness disarmed me. I had a feeling he wouldn't have been so forthcoming with other people—and that he was hiding a lot more pain than he was showing. "I'm so sorry."

"Me, too," he said. He lowered his head, hands resting

on the table on either side of his soda water. Neither of us had touched our drinks since he'd first spoken to me.

"He was a good kid," Nate continued. "Far too young to die."

"Did you see him after he left?" I wondered if that might make a difference.

"No. But he wrote every week. I wrote back, but based on the things he said in his letters, I don't think he ever got mine." My heart hurt hearing those words.

"Do you know what happened?"

Nate shook his head. "Just that he died honorably, and in battle. I have no idea where he was or what the battle was about."

That was true for so much of this war that had been troubling our nation for too many years now.

"What are you two talking about that's so all-fired serious?" Arnold shouted across the table, draining the last beer from his bottle. "Don't forget, man, she's a nun."

Nate switched gears to jest with his friends, and I smiled as the others teased him about an ego so big he thought he could get a nun, even laughed out loud when he joked back. And I felt like some kind of freak, missing half a body. It was time for me to go.

"The piano's calling, buddy!" Arnold said as he grabbed the second bottle of beer he'd ordered, not that I was counting. Nate stood and Arnold leaned toward me. "Nate plays here most Saturday nights when he's in town. Wait till you hear him."

I watched the six-foot-tall, perfectly proportioned, athletic man stroll to the piano, watched him wave as a couple of people called out to him. Watched his face break into an odd, almost peaceful smile. Even getting up to perform, there was nothing pretentious about Nate Grady.

And as he sat down, placed strong-looking fingers on the keys, I knew I couldn't leave yet. I'd be in trouble if I missed my ten o'clock curfew, but it was only a little past eight.

The first notes were muffled by the crowd, but by the time he'd reached his second stanza, the noise had stopped as everyone turned to listen. Nate played everything from current hits and love ballads to the big band forties songs I'd heard from my parents growing up. And he sang—in a voice so rich and deep I felt as though God was in every note.

I told myself I'd stay for one set. Long enough to tell him I thought he was wonderfully talented and to thank him for playing. I paid my bill so I'd be ready to go as soon as he finished. I still had time.

He broke into a rowdy rendition of "Great Balls of Fire" and before I knew it, I was laughing and cheering with the rest of the crowd. The break was good for me. And I loved the song. It had just hit number one, not that I'd ever really followed the pop charts. But that week I seemed to be more aware of everything worldly around me—maybe because I was looking at it all with an eye to leaving it behind.

After announcing a short break, Nate came back to

the table. Words of goodbye were forming on my lips. Someone had borrowed the chair he'd been using, but then he found another one and pulled it up next to mine. I *couldn't* just leave.

The guys were placing bets on which of the three jerks who'd been talking up a sweet young thing at the ski resort had won her favors for that night.

"She went home with her sister," Nate said dryly. "I saw them go."

"How d'you know she was her sister?" Arnold challenged in a good-natured way.

"She told me. She's getting married next week, and she and her sister, who's her maid of honor, went to Tahoe for a couple of days. It's their last time together as just the two of them."

Arnold and his pals were distracted when the waitress reappeared.

"Were you trying to get her to go out with you?" I asked Nate. My gall shocked me.

"I asked her if she was going to be all right leaving with those guys making such asses of themselves," he said just loudly enough for me to hear.

"Oh. That was a nice thing to do."

"It's habit. Girls skiing without a male escort seem to attract the worst kind of male attention."

He should know; he managed a ski resort. I couldn't help wondering how many managers watched out for the girls, and how many hit on them. More the latter, I expected.

A few minutes later, Nate excused himself to play again. Before he left, he asked if I'd be there during his next break. Without glancing at my watch, I nodded. I had about an hour.

The crowd slowly quieted as Nate played that second set, thinning out some, but not much. Couples swayed together on the dance floor. Chairs circled the piano. And then, just after nine-thirty, as Nate struck a new chord, he looked straight at me.

And started to sing.

"My Cup Runneth Over." He sang the whole song directly to me.

It didn't mean anything. How could it? We'd just met. He'd never seen me in the morning. Or any other time of day, for that matter.

And never would.

Still, I listened to every cadence, every lilt and syllable, and knew that this was a night I'd never forget.

"I have to go," I said, standing to put on my serviceable short black coat as he made his way back to the table. "I don't want to miss my curfew."

"I'll see you later," Nate told his friends, standing behind me. I wasn't sure what was going on until he followed me outside.

Nate walked me home. The couple of blocks had seemed insignificant when I'd traversed them with crowds of people earlier that evening. Now the quiet stretch of road, cloaked in the darkness of night, seemed far too intimate.

Nate kept a respectful distance, his jacketed arm not even bumping into mine.

"The guys told me about this cliff you skied today," I began. "They said you'd have won a medal if you'd been in the Olympics."

"In case you haven't figured it out, they exaggerate."

"But not many skiers make it over that particular drop-off upright, or so I hear."

"Plenty do. And plenty fall, too."

"How'd it feel, to be flying in the air like that? Were you scared?" I'd had butterflies in my stomach listening to Arnold talk about it.

"Truthfully?" He glanced down at me.

"Yeah."

"Anyone else would probably figure I'm crazy, but I have a feeling you're going to understand this. As soon as I started that run, I was so busy being aware of the wind gliding by—almost as though it was holding me up—and the crisp cold against my face, I didn't even think about landing until it happened. And then it was like any other slope. You do what you have to do to stay on your feet."

What he'd just described sounded like a moment of pure, spiritual bliss. Such intense involvement in the here-and-now that you were actually taken beyond it.

I'd petitioned to join a convent so I could learn how to have moments like that. There was something about this man, something deeper than anything I'd encountered in normal life, that was reaching out to me.

Almost as if he had answers to some of the mysteries I so desperately wanted to solve. Subconscious answers, maybe. But had them, just the same.

"I've enjoyed talking with you, Eliza Crowley," he said as we arrived at the heavy iron gate in front of St. Catherine's.

"And I'm glad I met you, Nate Grady." There didn't seem to be much harm in admitting that. I was never going to see him again.

"My flight back to Boulder leaves tomorrow evening," he said unexpectedly as I slipped through the gate and shut it behind me. "Any chance you could get away before then? Maybe we could take a walk."

Looking at him through the iron bars, all I could get out was, "I…"

"I'm sure you're on a pretty rigid schedule." He seemed to take pity on me. "It's okay if you can't. I won't be offended."

"I'm…I have…an hour free after lunch." I finally stumbled over the words. Who on earth was this woman uttering them? "We could meet down at the corner and walk through the gardens."

They weren't owned or tended by the sisters of St. Catherine's, but because the city park was so close, many of the sisters went there. I'd be in plain sight. Protected.

This could in no way be considered a date.

And until I moved out of college student housing into the main house, I was free to come and go. Curfew aside, of course.

"Great," he said. "What time?"

"One?"

"I'll be there."

I spent the next two hours lying awake in the long room I shared with seven other college students—three of them, like me, soon to be postulants—my nerves buzzing with energy and life. And with guilt… Going to that bar had been so completely out of character for me. And everything that had followed even more so.

My favorite fictional heroin flashed into my mind, a woman whose inner strength and sense of right and wrong had always spoken to me. My mother had read *Jane Eyre* to me as a child, and since then, I'd reread it often. Did the feelings I was trying so hard to comprehend bear any likeness to those experienced by Jane Eyre when she first met Mr. Rochester? I hoped not.

My attraction wasn't physical or romantic. At a time when I felt lost between past and future, when I was no more than an in-between, having left behind who I was and not yet arrived at who I was going to be, Nate Grady saw a *person*.

I wanted to talk to him one more time.

Chapter 2

One Sunday a month, the novices at St. Catherine's were permitted visits from their parents and siblings. That next day was one of those Sundays and with all the extra people milling around in the grounds, my departure went unnoticed. I wasn't required to stay on the premises—not until I moved from the dormitory—but on Sundays I rarely left, choosing to study with the sisters rather than involve myself in secular activities on God's day of rest.

Still, I wasn't doing anything *wrong* in meeting Nate and didn't really understand my relief at being able to escape unseen.

He was waiting at the entrance to the park, dressed

in dark slacks, a white shirt and long, skinny black tie. His hair was neatly parted and combed to one side.

"I feel kind of silly, shivering in this sweater while you're not even wearing your jacket." He'd slung it over his shoulder in a way that looked casual and rakish—sexy—at the same time. I rejected that thought immediately.

"It's nearly seventy degrees," he said, falling into step beside me without so much as an inappropriate glance at my knees, revealed by the navy plaid jumper I'd worn to Mass that morning. Granted, I was wearing my usual dark stockings. "I can't remember January ever being this warm. Not in my experience, anyway."

"One year, when I was about twelve, it hit ninety-five in January. My folks cooked hamburgers on the grill and all my older brothers and sisters were there. We played Marco Polo in the pool in our backyard."

"It's going to be about twenty-five degrees when I get home tonight."

His words stopped the smile on my lips—and calmed my heart. He would be leaving soon.

And I was never going to see him again.

"Did you bring anything memorable with you from Mass this morning?"

We'd been talking for almost an hour and I was beginning to feel as if Nate was an old friend. Still, the intimate query into my spiritual life threw me.

And yet it thrilled me. Other than the sisters, no one

had ever engaged me in conversation about this most personal aspect of my life.

I had no idea how to answer him.

"My Bible," I finally said, inanely.

"I meant from the sermon."

I glanced up at him, careful to lower my eyes before I met his. I wasn't yet under the tutelage that would require me to keep custody of my eyes, but I knew I would be soon. As a novice, I would be required to keep my gaze low, to refrain from direct eye contact. I wanted to practice it now, I told myself.

Either that, or I was afraid of liking him too much.

"Are you Catholic?" I asked him, instead of answering his question.

"I was born Catholic." He slid his hands in his pockets and we moved around a bend filled with brightly colored blossoms. "But I'm divorced and when the Church wouldn't recognize that, I felt kind of hypocritical staying. I'd done what I knew was right for me, but the Church expected me to remain in a marriage that wasn't working anymore."

I barely got through the rest of his words, stuck back in the *divorced* part.

"How long were you married?"

"Two years."

"When?"

"Before Keith shipped out."

A couple with two small children smiled at us. I felt

an urge to tell them that Nate and I *weren't* a couple, but held my tongue.

He'd been married at least four years ago. I would've been, at most, fifteen. "Why did you split up?"

"She was still at university and got involved in antiwar protests. Pretty soon they were consuming her life and I hardly saw her."

"She was protesting the war your little brother was fighting?"

Nate didn't say anything for a few minutes and I walked silently beside him.

"I never blamed her for her beliefs," he said slowly as we passed an elderly man walking a dog. "I supported her right to have them."

"So what happened?"

"She couldn't accept the fact that I wouldn't join her. Said she couldn't live with someone who promoted violence. About a year before Keith was killed, she left me for a fellow student and antiwar activist. They're married now and just had a baby."

"I'll bet she's got Dr. Spock's book," I said to cover my unexpected desire to comfort this man. I was completely out of my element. "He was indicted last week for conspiring to help others avoid the draft," I added when Nate said nothing.

"I hadn't heard that."

"I've been listening to the news a lot lately."

"Because you're interested or because you know you won't be able to after next week?"

Could the man see straight into my thoughts? My heart? That idea wasn't as threatening as it could have been.

"The latter, I'm afraid."

"There's absolutely nothing wrong with that."

"It feels…duplicitous."

"Wanting what you can't have, believing the grass is greener on the other side, is part of the human condition."

"You make it sound so…normal."

"It is," Nate said. "Listen, if it was easy to make the right choices, there'd be no glory in doing so."

His words made me think.

"You're a smart man, Nate Grady."

He chuckled. "I've made some pretty stupid decisions, that's all, and had to learn from them."

I wanted to know what each and every one of them was.

But I didn't dare ask.

We moved aside on the walkway to make room for a family dressed in church clothes. The son, about ten, I'd guess, had a stain on the knee of his slacks and his tie was askew. The little girl, with bows in her hair and lace on her socks, was pristine. The sight made me smile.

"You've never mentioned the rest of your family," I said. "Other than Keith."

"He was my only sibling."

"What about your parents? I imagine they took his death hard."

Hands still in his pockets, Nate slowed. "My father doesn't know. He took off right after Keith was born."

"You've never heard from him?"

"No."

"Have you ever tried to find him?"

"Nope. What was the point? He knew where we were. If he wanted contact, he knew how to get it." Nate didn't seem bitter. Or the least bit victimized, either.

I glanced sideways as we walked, trying to see his expression. "Aren't you curious about him?"

"Not really. I vaguely remember him. My mother said he never wanted kids and that made sense. He'd come and go as he pleased, and he never heard me when I talked to him. I don't think he loved my mom. They had to get married."

"Because of you?"

"Yeah." Nate nudged a stone off the cement with the toe of his shoe without missing a step. "I suppose he wasn't a bad guy. He didn't beat us or anything. Some people just aren't meant to be parents."

I thought the man sounded incredibly selfish.

"What about your mother?"

"She loved him."

As if that said it all.

"Do you see her often?"

"After our father left, she drank herself into liver disease and died ten years ago."

"So she didn't know about Keith."

"If the alcohol hadn't killed her, his death would have." Nate's voice was far calmer than mine would have been. "She drank a lot, but only after the two of us were in bed. Or out. She was a great mom, always there for us whenever she could be. She had no family support, which is why I think she fell into trouble with my father to begin with. Yet she raised two boys who knew they were loved, who never did drugs or got in trouble with the law. And she did it all on her own."

"In his sermon this morning, Father John talked about God's work in our society today," I said, returning without explanation to his earlier question. "He mentioned Jacques Cousteau's first undersea special on TV this past week. And the space-probe landing on the moon. Man's potential is limitless. But without God's help none of that could have happened."

"You say that as if you aren't sure you agree with him."

"I don't disagree," I said. "Not at all." Father John was a highly revered priest. I was a lowly postulant-to-be. "But I do think human choice and human will also contribute to scientific achievement. To *any* kind of achievement. What's the point of having a mind, of making choices, if we don't have the power to follow through on them?"

His nod encouraged me to continue. "Take your mother, for instance. She made choices. They didn't all work. But she took what she had and made good things happen."

"You're pretty smart for such a young woman." Nate's words were teasing, mocking my earlier comments about him. And yet, they held a note of admiration.

"You sound as though you're ancient," I teased him.

"Compared to you, I am."

I slid my hands into the sleeves of my sweater. "How old are you?"

"Thirty-three."

Fourteen years older than me. Which was safer than I'd thought.

"Say something."

"I'm surprised you even find me interesting." That didn't come out the way I'd meant it. I wasn't fishing for compliments.

"You've got a sense of peace about you," he said, pausing. "A kind of acceptance."

I certainly didn't see myself that way. But he had nothing to gain by turning my head. Our futures were clearly determined, and they'd be far from each other, with absolutely no point of connection.

"You aren't shallow." He started to walk again.

"Neither are you," I said, catching up with him.

"You have something I want," Nate said as we approached the entrance to the park and the moment I'd be saying goodbye to him forever.

I stopped breathing. And then my racing pulse forced air into my lungs.

I felt like running. But some impulse held me there, wouldn't let me go. "What?"

"A calm and knowing heart."

I almost wept. "Oh, Nate, if you could feel it right now, you wouldn't say that."

"You aren't afraid to face life, to confront your doubts and still head off full force."

"I'm scared to death!"

"On the surface, sure, but deep down?"

I glanced up only long enough to see the earnest question in his eyes. And without conscious thought, I entered my inner world, the mental space I flowed into when I meditated, looking for the sense of assurance that had always guided me. A world I trusted.

"Deep down I *am* content," I whispered, filled with gratitude at the fact he'd just pointed out to me. I hadn't consciously realized that my questions and confusions were only on the surface, and that inside, where it counted, I was calm. Peering up at him, I didn't care that tears fell from my eyes. I understood now what this weekend had been all about. God worked in mysterious ways. Sent messengers in a myriad of guises.

And at that moment I knew without question that Nate Grady was one of those messengers.

Chapter 3

I spent the rest of that day with Nate. I was a free woman—didn't have to be anywhere. The other soon-to-be postulants who were used to me hanging around the dormitory, studying or joining them in a game of croquet would be curious, but they wouldn't be disrespectful. Nate called and got a later flight back to Boulder. And we went to a little café not far from St. Catherine's and talked for hours. He saw so much more than most people did when they looked at daily life.

"Where'd you learn to play the piano?" I asked as dusk was starting to fall.

"Taught myself, mostly." We were drinking hot chocolate. "My grandparents bought a piano and I'd sit down and pick out songs. I didn't learn to read music until I was in high school."

"You'd just hear songs and sit down and play them?"

"Eventually." I loved Nate's grin.

"If you heard a song right now for the first time, could you play it?"

"Probably."

I wondered about that morning's sermon—wondered where man's talents were strictly his own and where God was responsible for them.

"I enjoy skiing," Nate said. "And I love working with the kids all summer. But playing the piano...completes me."

I understood what he meant by that. "I'm not sure I know what completes me."

"Giving your life to the service of God?"

"Can it be that broad?" I frowned. "Shouldn't there be some talent that's more personally my own?"

"I don't know." His gaze was steady. Sincere. "What I can tell you, what I've learned, is that the more rules you place on whatever you're looking for, the less likely you are to find it."

He'd given me something else to think about.

"Like if someone spent his whole life searching for some grand purpose, he'd miss the fact that he was a great gardener and that his flowers brought comfort to hundreds of people."

"Or the proverbial janitor whose smile touched hundreds of kids over the years..."

His words faded and we smiled at each other. An easy, comfortable communication between like spirits. I was glad I'd met him.

"You're sure you won't be in trouble for spending so much time with me?"

We were heading in the general direction of the convent. It was almost completely dark and I hugged my navy cardigan more closely around my body.

"While I'm living in the dormitory, I pretty much come and go as I please," I told him. "Other than curfew, and a few rules like no food in the rooms and no male visitors, I don't have restrictions."

"Why no food?"

"The sisters are notoriously clean." A trait I shared with them.

"No male visitors—has it been that way for all your college years?"

"There've only been two and a half of them." I was feeling a little nervous about getting back, missing my Sunday-evening time with the other postulants-to-be. And yet, I hated to see the end of these hours with my in-between friend. "I took college classes while I was still in high school. But yes, it's been that way the whole time."

"Did you date in high school?"

"A little. Not much. Boys bored me."

Except for him. But then Nate was a man—fourteen years my senior. There was nothing boyish about him.

And it was fully dark outside. Would the sisters be hugely disappointed in me if they could see me now?

"When did you know you wanted to be a nun?"

"I've felt drawn to the convent my entire life. I went to Catholic schools and have been visiting St. Catherine's since I was in high school. Joining the order was a natural progression. But because it's a teaching order, I needed to get my degree."

"So you won't always be living as secluded a life as you will for the next few years?"

I could see the corner far ahead where I'd turn to go home and started to relax again. I was almost there.

"Seclusion ends when I take my vows." It felt as good tonight to be talking to him about what was to come as it had the night before. "The point of being a postulant and then a novice is to leave the world behind so I can fully concentrate on my spiritual life. I'll develop self-discipline and spend a lot of time in contemplation of God and the vows I mean to take. I won't associate with many people, except for others in my position."

"Not even the nuns?"

"Except for those who oversee us, no."

We were only a block away from saying goodbye forever.

"Can people come and visit you?"

"One Sunday a month and only immediate family."

"What about letters?"

"I'll be permitted to write one a week to my parents,

but it'll be read by the sisters and any letters my family sends will also be read."

He didn't say anything and I was afraid. It was important to me that he understand, that he not judge my choice too harshly. Though why his opinion mattered I didn't know.

"I won't be a prisoner, Nate," I told him. "The rules aren't there to confine me, but to protect me from the world so I can prepare myself for the life I've chosen. Or—perhaps—to figure out that this isn't for me. The sisters work very hard to help us clear the voices from our minds so we might hear the inner guide inside us."

"Would that everyone had that chance." His softly spoken words quieted my heart.

"Would you hate me if I told you I wish I'd met you in another time and place?"

I'd entered the grounds—closed the heavy iron gate behind me. The drive, which had been lined with cars earlier that day, was now deserted. Silent. Dimly lit. Before I could take another step, his words reached me.

I turned back to see Nate standing with both hands clutching the black metal. And lost the battle I'd been fighting with tears since my hastily muttered goodbye— my wish for him to have a safe and happy life.

"Where and when would that be?" I whispered.

"Anywhere I go, I'll be who I am right now." A woman who was bound for a life of poverty and chastity. "And you'll still be fourteen years older than me, living in another world."

"I will never forget you."

"Nor I you."

I walked away then. Because it was the right thing to do. I trusted that, deep inside, it was what I wanted to do. I would miss Nate, but I hardly knew him. I was committed to God.

My tears continued to fall long into the night—and I asked forgiveness for shedding them.

On Thursday, having spent four days cloistered in my room, at confession, at Mass or in prayer, I shared a silent lunch with several of the other candidates who'd be joining the order with me the following week. Afterward, back at the dormitory, I found a letter waiting in my cubicle.

Assuming it was from my sister June in Cincinnati— she was the only one who ever wrote me—I tossed it onto my cot. On its way down, the bold, virtually illegible writing that served as a return address caught my eye.

My sister's writing was small. She always printed.

Sick to my stomach I sat beside the envelope, staring at it. I shoved my hands beneath my thighs. A white, sheetlike curtain separated my area from the other six cubicles in the long room, but the privacy it offered wasn't necessary at the moment. I was the only one there. The rest of the girls were on the lawn playing volleyball.

I'd thought of Nate often that week. And repented

afterward—each and every time. I still believed he'd been heavensent, to show me that my confusion and questions were momentary and my soul was content. I also feared he might be my temptation.

A few nights before, very late, I'd awakened from a dream about Nate—and lain there wondering what it would feel like to be hugged by him. To be kissed… I'd been afraid to go back to sleep in case I dreamed of him again.

He'd shown me the inner peace I possessed, yet it had remained elusive since the moment I'd turned my back and walked away from him.

I understood that this was one of life's contradictions. That human need to want what you can't have, as he'd described it. Was this a test of my resolve? I wondered.

My mind would not be quiet.

The envelope had to be dealt with. I could throw it in the trash. Perhaps that was how I passed this test.

But what if he had something to say that I needed to know? Some insight or revelation that would bring clarity back to my heart. What if he was sick? Or injured?

He'd never shown any inclination to be anything but proper with me. Our association was a moment in a lifetime—there, and then gone. We'd been brought together to strengthen each other, I told myself, to bless each other's lives, and then move on. Only my obsessive inability to let go of my earthly thoughts was a problem.

I picked up the envelope.

I was not going to tarnish the gift of Nate's brief friendship with the dark side of human nature. Of *my* nature.

After waiting until my stomach felt calm, I slit open the envelope. Two sheets of folded paper slid out. There was writing only on the inside, but through the paper I could see that he'd written more than one paragraph.

Looking around to make sure I was still alone, I unfolded the long sheets.

My dearest Eliza,

My heart skipped a beat as I read the greeting. I *wasn't* his. But it felt good to read the words, anyway— as though I had a special, sacred friend. A friendship outside the boundaries and beliefs that defined my life. Outside the opinions and judgments of others.

My hands were shaking so hard it took me another second to be able to focus on the next words.

Please forgive my intrusion. I have struggled with myself since leaving you at the convent gate on Sunday night, knowing that when I walked away it had to be forever. And yet something inside me compels me to contact you, to speak of my heart, and let fate, or your God, or whatever powers that be take us wherever they must.

The rest of the world faded away and I read on as though my entire being rested on these next moments.

Had you known me more than a day, you'd know that I'm a man who always thinks before he leaps. I carefully plan before I step. There's a reason for everything I do, and I'm aware of the reason before I do it.

Until now. I have no idea why I feel I have to write this letter, but I won't rest until it's done.

I don't have an explanation for what I'm about to do and have no way to convince you that I'm fully sane as I sit here. I know only what I know and it is this:

I love you. I believe you are my soulmate. I would give this more time, not to convince myself of the rightness of what I'm feeling, or because I have any doubt, but to give you time to know me more completely. I would attempt to court you according to societal expectations, except that in one short week you will be lost to me. I know that once you make a commitment, you make it fully.

In this untraditional and inadequate way, I must ask, *Will you marry me, Eliza Crowley?*

I read those words and can't believe I'm doing this. You have me so tangled up I hardly know myself.

And as I consider what I'm asking, I must, in all fairness, tell you about myself. I have a temper, but most times have pretty good control over it. I cannot promise not to get angry with you. Nor can I promise to make every moment for the rest of your life a happy one. I can't assure you that I won't ever make you angry or disappoint you. I *can* tell you that I'll try always to listen to both sides and to consider you fairly in every decision I make.

I can also promise that I will love you until the day I die and beyond.

I don't say any of this to pressure you. I do not intend to contact you again, or to try in any way to convince you to accept my proposal. As I said, I believe you are my soulmate but don't know if we're meant to be together in this lifetime. If not, I will wait until we meet again.

Yours,

Nathanial Grady

Joy unlike any I'd experienced before coursed through my body. It was followed by a sense that something in my life had just settled into rightness.

The sensation lasted about ten seconds, until my eyes focused on the letter and I read it a second time. It was a fairy tale, better than most of the stories my mother had read to me when I was a child—with the exception, maybe, of *Jane Eyre*.

It was the stuff that dreams and magic—not lives—were made of. Like my association with Nate, it was a moment, not solid, not sustainable.

I couldn't possibly marry him. I didn't even have to ask myself before I knew the answer to that. I'd committed myself to vows of chastity. I truly wanted the life I'd chosen for myself.

But even if this episode with Nate was supposed to show me that I wasn't meant for the convent, I still couldn't marry him. No matter how badly I wanted to. He'd been divorced.

If I were to marry Nate, I wouldn't only have to leave the convent, I'd have to leave the Church.

If I was going to seriously consider this proposal, I would have requested counsel from the Mistress of Postulants, but I was in no doubt as to my response. It wasn't uncommon to have a trial present itself just before entering into the religious life. This was a test of my faith, no more.

Leaving Nate's letter on the thin, hard mattress, I sat in the plain chair at my small writing table, picked up pen and paper, and started to write. He'd said he wouldn't contact me again and I knew he wouldn't, whether I replied to his letter or not. But it wouldn't be kind to leave him hanging. He'd given his heart to me. I wanted to explain to him what was in mine.

And then I'd put the interlude behind me and focus on the life that was to come.

I got as far as *Dear Nate* before I began to cry. When I was finished, I dropped my pen, reread what I'd written and started to shake.

There was only one sentence.

Yes, I'll marry you.

Chapter 4

I had a telegram from Nate the following Thursday. He was flying in to see me for a few hours on Friday afternoon. He told me what time to expect him—and nothing else.

Holding the only book in my possession that was almost as dog-eared as my Bible, my mother's copy of *Jane Eyre*, I hugged it to my chest that night—thinking about the next day.

Had Nate changed his mind? He'd probably never expected me to accept his crazy proposal.

Or did he think he was coming to take me away forever? I couldn't go. I was only a semester away from my teaching degree.

I was scared to death to see him again. And I was so excited at the thought of his arrival that I couldn't concentrate on my studies.

Dressed in jeans and a hand-knit pullover, I was waiting nervously at the convent gates when he arrived.

Afraid that he was going to pull me into his arms, and that I wouldn't know how to respond, I was surprised— and a little disappointed if the truth be told—when he just stood there, looking at me as though he'd be content to do that for the rest of his life.

"I don't own any makeup."

This is the first thing I say to the man I've agreed to marry!

"You're beautiful without it. Genuine."

Had he looked at me that way the previous weekend? I hadn't noticed. But then, I'd avoided his gaze more than I'd met it. A sister kept custody of her eyes.

That heavy weight was back in my stomach. It had been there constantly since I'd mailed my letter to Nate the week before. I wasn't ever going to be a nun.

Only the sisters and Nate knew that. Only Nate knew why.

"Are you scared?"

I nodded. I was still on my side of the open gate.

"You don't have to do this."

"I want to."

"Are you sure?"

Standing there so close to him, mesmerized by his loving expression, I nodded again. "It's just that I've been planning to become a nun for as long as I can remember and now I realize—"

"What?"

"I don't know how to be anything else."

Nate reached for my hand and gently tugged me onto the other side. "You aren't what you do, Eliza," he said while I was busy experiencing something like butterflies at the very first touch of his warm skin against mine. "You're already who you are. Whether you add the role of sister or wife or even mother to that, you are still the sweet, gentle spirit you were when you came to this earth."

Mother. My heart raced. I'd been so consumed by what I was leaving behind, and contemplating with nervous excitement the idea of lying in Nate's arms, I hadn't considered the possible outcome of that act. This was all happening so fast….

"Do you want to have children?" I asked.

"I'd like to, yes. But if you don't—"

"I do." I cut him off, suddenly so embarrassed I could hardly stay there with him. A week ago I was planning to go to my grave chaste and here I was standing on the sidewalk talking about having sex with a man. And while I knew the physical basics, that was *all* I knew on that particular subject. Not much point in teaching intricate details—or having "the talk"—with a girl who's going to be a nun.

I looked down, afraid he'd seen the sudden redness on my cheeks.

"Hey." With one finger beneath my chin, he lifted my gaze to his. "Your plans to enter the convent rushed our courtship, but the rest of it we'll take as slowly as you need to," he said, embarrassing me further. "Do you understand?"

I tried to act nonchalant. "You're a grown man, Nate. You've been married before. You're used to—" I couldn't do it. "You know…"

The convent was looming on my left, filling my peripheral vision.

"I'm a man, not an animal." His words were soft with an understanding of something I didn't understand at all. I wondered if he guessed just how little experience I had.

And worried that, once he found out, he'd regret this rash impulse.

"You're a beautiful woman, Eliza," he continued, and I was relieved when he started to walk. "But that's not why I wrote to you. I want to spend the rest of my life with the person I met last weekend. I want to feel the way I felt when I was with you. And while I'm looking forward to our physical relationship, I intend to give you all the time you need to adjust to that aspect of our life together. Okay?"

"Yes," I whispered, wondering how long that would be. A year? Maybe two?

He was walking beside me as he had the weekend before, not touching me at all. I kind of wanted to feel my hand inside his again—and thought maybe I'd like him to keep it there.

"I've only got a few hours before I have to go back—can't be gone two weekends in a row during the busy season—but I came as soon as I got your letter. To make plans. Have you told your parents yet?"

"No."

"Have you told anyone?"

I hadn't known what to do. I'd answered a letter, but I had no idea what Nate's intentions were. Or if he would've changed his mind by the time he got my reply.

"I spoke to the Mistress of Postulants. I didn't tell her about…us…only that I didn't feel I could enter the convent anymore."

Even if I'd never heard from Nate again, that much had become clear.

We walked to the park and then inside, passing a woman dressed in jeans and a purple sweater holding the hand of a curly-haired blond toddler dressed the same. A young black woman pushed a baby carriage past us. An elderly man wearing an unzipped beige windbreaker sat on the bench just inside the entrance. I noticed them all. And the vividness of the green grass, the trees that were still bare now, the velvety magnolia blossoms.

"How long do you have before you need to be out of your room?"

"I'm at college on full scholarship, so I'm free to stay in the dorm until I graduate in June. You don't have to be committed to the convent to live there, you just have to be willing to follow the rules."

The sky was bluer today than it had been in a while.

The sun brighter. Yet nothing seemed familiar. Because I'd changed?

"That gives us a few months."

"I have to graduate." I clung to that goal as though it was all that was left of me. Certainly it was the only part of myself I recognized at the moment.

"Of course you do," Nate said, and I think that's when I fell completely, irrevocably in love with him. Until then, my heart had ached to be with him, to bless his life in any way I could, but it had felt like a big risk to take. A perilous thing to do.

Now it felt safe.

Contrary to what my head might have been telling me, the words I'd written to Nate Grady the week before were not retractable.

On January 22 of that year, *Rowan and Martin's Laugh-In* premiered on NBC. And I had a letter from Nate. He wanted to know if July 20th would be an acceptable date for the wedding. Camp would be between sessions the following week and would be closed, giving us time for a brief honeymoon and to get me settled in.

I visited my parents that evening. Nate had offered to go with me when he was in town, but I hadn't wanted to share my brief time with him.

Late that night, I wrote him and said that July 20th would be fine. And that I'd like to get married in Colorado.

I didn't tell him then that my parents had just disowned me.

* * *

On February 8th state police officers killed three black students engaged in an antiwar demonstration at South Carolina State. Nate called me three times that week. We talked about the Orangeburg massacre, as the attack was being called. About his brother. And he had some good news. He'd found a house he wanted to buy for us. I told him that if he liked it, it was fine with me. In truth, anywhere with Nate was going to be heaven as far as I was concerned.

Once I got past the initial wifely duty, that is. Nate and I still had not kissed. But I'd been doing some reading about the mating process and while I was trying to keep an open mind, I was pretty well scared out of my wits.

Charlotte Brontë had skipped the intimate details with Jane and Mr. Rochester.

March 1st was the day Johnny Cash married June Carter. I wanted the marriage to work, but I didn't think it would. He was such a rebel, probably even did drugs, and everyone knew June was just a darling.

Nate called the next day. I wasn't in a good frame of mind, missing him, and feeling so alone, since I no longer had either my family or the sisters to turn to.

I tried to explain my feelings but knew I'd failed miserably when he asked, "Are you having second thoughts?"

"No. Not at all." Surprisingly, I wasn't. "The one thing that seems to be a constant in my life these days is my certainty about marrying you."

"You're sure of that?"

I couldn't tell if he was feeling insecure, or just trying to make certain I was all right.

"Absolutely."

"Because if you're having second thoughts, we need to talk about them, Eliza."

"I'm not!" I was beginning to get irritated with his unwillingness to believe me. Which was testament to how out of sorts I felt. Generally I was a very patient person.

"It's to be expected," he said. "You're young and I rushed you."

I got cold then. "Nate, are you trying to tell me *you've* changed your mind?"

"No." It was a good thing his response was so unequivocal, otherwise I might've become completely unraveled. "But I've had a few more years to find out exactly what I want, which enables me to recognize it when I find it."

"And you think I don't know my own mind?" Did he have as little faith in me as my parents?

"Oh, Eliza, I'm sorry." His sigh was long and deep.

"Are you going to tell me what's wrong?" I asked.

"Nothing's wrong. I've been thinking too much and knotted myself up, that's all. I just needed to hear your voice."

"Well, I'd like to hear what you were thinking about," I said.

"It's late and you have class tomorrow. It wasn't important. Can't we leave it at that?"

"No." I had an instinct about this.

"I'd rather not get into it. At least not now, on the phone."

I'd figured as much. "That's why I'm pretty sure I should hear about it."

He sighed again. I leaned against the wall, holding the pay phone so tightly my hand was starting to cramp. That phone in the dark hallway of our dorm was the only one on which we could receive calls.

"It's not a big deal, Eliza."

"So you keep saying."

"I don't want you upset or jumping to conclusions."

My skin was clammy and I was half-afraid I might throw up. "Tell me."

"I wasn't married just once."

My only coherent thought was that he'd said his news wasn't important. Whether I was incredulous that he could think that, or hoping I'd misunderstood, I couldn't say.

"We were young," Nate said a few seconds later. "Too young. It didn't last long. A couple of months. Her parents were moving to New Jersey and we figured if we didn't get married, we'd never see each other again."

"How...young?" I could hardly speak.

"Eighteen."

Wow. I had no idea how to react to this.

"Say something."

"I'm not...I don't—" Helpless, I just stood there clutching the phone, letting the wall support me.

"Tell me what you're feeling."

"Deflated. Like I'm not sure I know you as well as I thought."

"I've lived thirty-two years, Eliza," he said, his voice taking on a weary note. "There are many facts about me, things I've experienced, that you don't know yet. But none of them change who I am. They're things that happened—"

"A marriage is more than something that just *happened*."

"This one wasn't. We never had a life together, never even set up house. We lived with my mother for the couple of months it lasted."

I was tired. Needed a good night's rest. "You said you got twisted up in thought." I returned to our earlier conversation. "Were you afraid you were making the same mistake twice? Getting married before you were ready?"

"No." He actually chuckled. "I was afraid you were."

Considering what he'd told me, I supposed I could understand that. Maybe. "I'm not a child living at home with my parents." Quite the opposite, in fact.

"I know that."

"Then please don't treat me like one."

"I love you, Eliza Crowley."

"I love you, too."

I just wished love didn't have to be so hard.

As timing would have it, my oldest sister, Alice, had me paged in the dorm one evening the next week. She'd been sent by my parents to talk me out of my madness and spent a full hour telling me everything wrong with a man she'd never even met.

"He's divorced, Liza!"

I certainly couldn't argue with that.

"You'll have to leave the Church!"

I couldn't argue with that, either.

And when she told me that if I went through with the wedding she and my other two sisters, like my parents, would be unable to participate in my life, I didn't debate the issue.

I cried myself to sleep instead.

Two weeks later, Robert Kennedy announced his campaign for president of the United States and Rome indicated that while it deplored the concept of rock and roll Masses, it wouldn't prohibit them. I read the news with an almost clinical detachment. Once I married Nate, I would no longer be attending Mass of any kind. I'd be married to a divorced man—a union the Church refused to recognize. And like Nate, I saw no point in worshipping within a society to which I could not belong.

I would miss attending mass.

But my God I'd take with me.

Putting down the newspaper, I went out to the hall, dropped a dime into the phone and dialed my brother, William, at his apartment in Los Angeles. I asked if he'd give me away at my wedding.

He agreed!

* ★ *

North Vietnam agreed to meet with the United States for preliminary peace talks during the first days of April—something I paid careful attention to now that I loved Nate and knew about Keith. And on the fourth day of that month, Martin Luther King was shot in the neck with a single bullet while standing on the balcony outside his room at the Lorraine Motel in Memphis. Crying, not understanding the injustice of a good man's life ending in such a senseless way, I called Nate. He couldn't make sense of the tragedy any more than I could, but talking to him helped just the same. I mentioned that my brother would be giving me away at our wedding and finally told him that my parents and sister would not be attending. It seemed like such a small thing at that point.

On April 18th Great Britain sold the London Bridge to a United States oil company that would be erecting it in Arizona. I wasn't sure why Arizonans wanted a British bridge, but I liked the idea of bridges being raised far from their homes. I hoped that symbolism would apply to me, too.

The next day, walking back from class, I turned onto the block of the convent gate and saw Nate standing there, his face at once welcoming and somewhat grim.

I flew to him, almost dropping my books, and my whole being felt as though it was soaring as he grabbed me up, books and all, into a full-bodied hug. Glancing up, tears in my eyes and a smile on my lips, I meant to ask him why he was there, how long he could stay, why he hadn't told me he was coming. I kissed him instead.

Just like that. With no thought. No worries about how to do it. My mouth went straight to his. In that moment, it no longer mattered that I'd lost most of my family, my church, all sense of security. I'd found the home I wanted for the rest of my life.

"I only have tonight," Nate was saying several minutes later as we walked toward the pub where we'd first met. I'd brought my books inside, told my roommates not to expect me until curfew and hurried back to him without even changing out of my plaid jumper and white blouse. At least I'd grabbed my navy sweater for when the sun went down.

He was holding my hand—hadn't let go since I'd come back out from the convent—and now he squeezed it. "I want to meet your folks."

Oh. My spirits plummeted. "If we've only got a few hours, Nate," I said, keeping my voice light, "I want to spend them with you—alone."

"You love your parents," he argued. "I'm not going to be the cause of a rift between you. I'd like to meet them, talk to them, assure them that I'm honorable and want only what's best for you."

"They won't listen."

"By your own admission, all they want is for you to be happy."

That used to be true—when I was still a member of their church. When they thought I was in my right mind. In their view, they weren't cutting off their support to punish me; they were doing what they thought was best, refusing to go along with my harebrained idea because they believed that their rejection would bring me to my senses. And the hardest part was that I understood—which made it impossible to hate them.

Only to grieve their loss.

"We can take a cab out to their house," Nate said, "and if all goes well, have a late dinner before I catch my plane back."

"We can't."

"Of course we can."

"They won't see you, Nate."

"What do you mean, they won't see me? They don't even know me."

"I know them."

He stopped by a pay phone outside the pub. Pulled change from his pocket. "Call them."

"It won't do any good."

"Humor me."

Because I loved him so much, I complied. I knew the effort was wasted.

And still, I had to take an extra second in the glass-enclosed booth after the call, collecting myself before I could face Nate. I'd had no idea my father had so much coldness in him.

"Well?" Nate asked, standing with both hands on his hips, facing me.

I shook my head. Hoped that would be the end of it.

"They aren't home?"

I couldn't start our life together with lies.

"They said that if we go there, they'll call the cops."

I would never forget the look on Nate's face.

Chapter 5

In May, Vietnamese peace talks began in Paris, *Mission: Impossible* won an Emmy Award and I graduated from college. Nate came to the ceremony. And so did my brother, William. The two men—eight years apart in age—were as wary of each other as prowling tigers. But that night Nate played piano at the pub again and during the second set William asked me to dance.

"He's talented," my older brother said to me as we moved slowly around the crowded floor.

"Yeah."

"He's not shallow."

"I know."

"He loves you."

I got choked up at that.

"And you love him, don't you?"

"Very much."

William didn't say any more about Nate and me after that, but when the break came, he bought a round of drinks. And by the time I had to be back at the convent dormitory, where I'd be staying until July as a summer student, taking a first-session graduate class, the two men were discussing baseball homerun records and an outfielder who'd played 695 games straight.

I'd never been a fan of the sport, but I was going to love it from then on.

Robert F. Kennedy was killed in early June. People everywhere were shocked, horrified that the assassination of prominent people was now part of our reality. We'd suffered two of them in two months.

At a time when I was taking a blind leap away from everything familiar and safe, my country was in turmoil. I wondered what God thought of how we were treating His world. I wondered if I'd ever feel safe again.

Consumed by fear—more menacing in itself than anything else—I squared my shoulders and requested counsel from Sister Michael Damien, the Mistress of Postulants. Had I entered the convent she would have been my mentor, training me in proper decorum, regulations and spiritual matters.

I hadn't spoken with her since I'd told her I would

not be entering the convent, the day after I'd answered Nate's first letter.

I was in awe of her and intimidated beyond measure.

"Thank you for seeing me," I said quietly, eyes downcast as I sat with her on a warm cement bench during the postulant recreation time after lunch.

Her gown rustled beside me and I felt her soft palm cover the knot my hands had become in my lap. "We've known each other a long time, my dear. You're always welcome."

I wished so badly that would continue to be true. Despite my excitement over the future, a future I'd sacrificed everything to have, my heart ached for what I was leaving behind.

The postulants were playing a rousing game of basketball not too far away. I could hear them. And, in that moment, envied them. Two of my dormitory sisters were there, too.

"I'm getting married."

"I guessed as much."

My eyes darted up at that, meeting the serene blue of hers. "You did?"

"There are only two reasons a young woman as committed as you were decides against taking her vows," she said. "Either she finds that her heart's direction was not true, or she finds a man whose pull is stronger than the Church. I have no doubt your heart is true."

"That makes me sound weak. Disloyal."

"Not at all, my dear. It makes you alive."

"Do you think less of me?"

"For following your heart? I do not."

"Then why do I feel like I'm turning traitor to my calling? I love him—so much—but I feel as though I haven't been true to my purpose for being on earth."

"Let me ask you this, Eliza. Do you *think* you're being untrue to yourself? Or do you *know* you are?"

"I'm so confused at the moment, I'm not even sure I could tell the difference."

"Tell me why you're doing this. Leaving the life you'd chosen in order to marry this man."

"Because I have to." I answered without analyzing. And then heard what I'd said. "Not…*have* to," I quickly explained. "He asked me and even though I tried, I couldn't say no. I listen to my parents, to my sister, and my head knows that much of what they say is correct. I understand their fears for me. I cry myself to sleep at night because I miss them. And still, I can't tell Nate that I won't marry him."

"Why not?"

"I feel I have to do this." I gave that worthless answer because it was all I had.

"Ahhh."

Sister Michael Damien's smile was kind—and knowing.

"What?"

"You *feel*," she said. "That, my dear child, is your heart speaking. Your head is confusing you, but you're being guided by the inner knowing that will always direct you. It brought you here to us for a time, for a purpose, and now your heart will lead you elsewhere, for the next stage of your journey."

I wasn't sure I understood.

"But how can marrying Nate be my calling if it takes me away from service to the God who made me?"

And this was the crux of my dilemma. I *was* going to marry Nate. But did that mean I'd be less than I was born to be? Less righteous? Less loving and spiritual? Less Godly?

Was I a spineless creature? Giving in to earthly pleasure because I wasn't strong enough to sacrifice for a greater purpose?

"When a girl is deciding between the life of a nun or a life of marriage and family, Eliza, there is no better or worse. No choice more righteous than the other. God needs dedicated wives and mothers just as badly as He needs Sisters. Mothers are the core of family life, and family is the core of God's work. Both callings serve Him equally—a mother in a more intimate setting and a Sister in a broader way."

It was as though the sun had come out from behind a cloud.

"My calling is to serve God, but to do it in a different capacity than I first envisioned?"

"I believe so. Yes."

I was elated, relieved—and then stopped short.

"What if he's been married before?"

"He's a widower?"

"Divorced."

Sister Michael Damien didn't say a word. And a few minutes later, when I stood to go, her concerned gaze followed me down the walk.

The day I got married, Jane Asher broke her engagement to singer Paul McCartney on live television.

Nate and I had a small wedding at the home of his friend and boss, resort owner Walt Blackwell, and as I was changing into my short, simple white dress that evening, Walt's oldest daughter, Mary, told me about Asher and McCartney. I was pretty sure she was hoping I'd follow Jane's example, minus the television crew. Walt and his family didn't seem all that happy about me as Nate's bride.

"Nate and your brother just arrived," Mary said, taking the sponge rollers out of my hair. The squishy little tubes were the only curlers my short strands could fit around, and I'd had them in all afternoon. I hadn't seen Nate since he'd picked me up from the airport and dropped me at the Blackwell home.

A door opened off the hall outside the guest suite where I'd spent most of the day with the myriad people Nate had hired to help me get ready for my wedding.

"Be happy for me, Walt." All my senses came alive at the sound of Nate's voice in the hall. Since the moment I'd met him, I'd craved his presence.

"She's nineteen, son."

"Soon to be twenty." The voices came closer as the men passed our door.

Mary's hand stilled, holding a strand of my hair straight up.

"A child," Walt said.

"She's already finished college and certified to teach."

"I just hate to see you go through what you did when Karen left." Walt's voice was kind, fatherly and growing fainter.

"Trust me, Walt, Eliza isn't like Karen."

"She's a kid with nothing looking to you for security."

"She comes from a working-class family, but I wouldn't say they've got nothing. Besides, she had her life settled, had more security than most of us will ever have, before I came along."

"And offered her a better way of life."

"I love her." Nate's voice grew in intensity, making it easily heard, and I tried not to cry.

"Are you sure you aren't just itching to get her in the sack and marriage is the only way to do that?"

The voices faded before I could hear Nate's reply.

"My father thinks we're downstairs already."

My eyes met Mary's in the mirror. Hers were filled with pity. Mine with tears.

Twenty minutes later, as I entered the beautifully decorated living room on my brother's arm, I saw that Arnold had flown in for the wedding. My high school friend, his sister Patricia, was with him. I'd had no idea she was coming and seeing her there with the dozen or so other people sitting in rented chairs made me start to cry again. I remembered the silly high school game we'd played, writing notes back and forth as though we were the characters in Brontë's novel. We'd both loved that book and it gave us a private, and I think creative, way to express our feelings. I'd always been Jane—because I was the one who'd go against the crowd. She'd been different characters, the tragic Helen, who'd died of consumption. Or the lovely Blanche Ingram. Or even the first Mrs. Rochester.

Looking at her now, I couldn't remember a time I'd been so emotionally on edge.

And then I saw Nate standing beside the minister, flanked by gorgeous white lilies, and as our eyes met, the rest of the room—the rest of the world—faded away. If I was crazy for doing this, I prayed the craziness would last forever.

After a champagne toast, a few photos and a bite of cake, Nate and I left our small celebration to drive up to a cabin Walt owned in the mountains not far from Boulder. We would be there until Monday.

"The bathroom's down that hall," Nate said, my small suitcase in one hand and his duffel in the other. I stood just inside the door of the dimly lit main room, still wearing my white dress, watching as he disappeared behind another door at the far end—and returned without either bag.

I'd known we were going to be sleeping together, of course. We were husband and wife now. But in recent days I hadn't let myself think about what that actually *meant*—or picture it really happening.

For the first time I could remember in my life, I wasn't prepared.

I thought briefly about claiming my monthly cycle as an excuse—but immediately dismissed the idea. I couldn't start my life with Nate on a lie.

Nor could I really see myself talking to him about such an intimate topic.

"Can I get you something?" He'd taken off his jacket and tie, but still wore the shiny black wing tip shoes.

A ride back to the city? I stared at him.

"Don't look at me like that."

"Like what?"

"Like I'm going to eat you alive."

I fidgeted, but didn't run and hide the way I wanted to. "I'm just a little nervous…"

I backed up a step as he approached. Nate slowed, but continued toward me, reaching for my hand.

"We'll take things slowly," he said, his head slightly bent and tilted to the right, as though to get a better view into my skittish eyes. Walking me over to the couch, Nate sat and pulled me gently down beside him, arms around me as he held me against his chest.

I liked it there. A lot. Or I would have if I'd thought I could stay just that way for the rest of my life.

"I wish I could tell you it won't hurt the first time." I was glad for the low light then as my face suffused with heat. "But for women, it usually does."

I'd read about that. And couldn't imagine why any woman would welcome that kind of pain.

"It's only for a second, though, and then the feeling's so incredible, Eliza, there's nothing that compares to it."

I'd read that, too. Just wasn't sure I believed it. Most of the information I'd found had been written by men. Doctors.

"I told you we'd take all the time you need," he murmured. I'd wondered if he'd remember that. "We don't have to do this tonight." He didn't sound the least put out with me.

"No, that's okay." I wanted to get it over with. "I'm just not…" I had to stop, take a deep breath. "I don't know what I'm supposed to do, exactly."

"Your mother didn't have a talk with you when you were younger?"

"I was going to be a nun."

And since I'd made the decision to leave the convent, my mother hadn't spoken to me.

He shifted, took my hand and placed it over the zipper of his slacks. I wanted to die. And to move my fingers, too. I was curious. I wanted to know what Nate felt like.

I wanted the privilege of sharing something with Nate that no one else could share, of seeing parts of him no one else was allowed to see.

"This is what happens to me when I think about making love to you," Nate said. "A woman's desire is not so obvious, but it can be just as intense. Our job, yours and mine, is to help you feel it. That's all."

It couldn't be all. Even I knew you didn't make babies with only feeling.

"Until your eagerness matches mine, we go no further."

I glanced up at him, not nearly so embarrassed as he sat there letting me touch him in his most private place. I guess I should've been embarrassed. More so, even. But I wasn't.

"How do we do that? How do we make sure I feel it, too?"

He swelled more beneath my hand and my fingers wrapped around him. He was throbbing.

"We could go in the bedroom and lie down," he said. "Fully clothed."

When he added that last part, I started to relax a little. And to tense with a strange kind of anticipation at the same time.

"Okay."

He stood and I was disappointed as my hand slid away. Would he put it back when we got to the bedroom?

I hoped so as, hand in his, I followed him.

Nate lay down first, settled me against him, almost exactly like we'd been on the couch, except now our bodies were side by side. His hip pressed into my stomach right about where the scar was from when I had my appendix out. Our thighs were touching.

"I'd like to kiss you."

"Okay."

"I mean really kiss you."

I wasn't sure what that meant. We'd kissed every time we were together, ever since that first time outside the convent. "Okay."

Shifting enough for our faces to be level, Nate touched his lips to mine. I kissed him back, the sensation familiar, pleasant, reassuring. And then it changed. His lips opened, and his tongue was there, running lightly along my lips, tickling them.

I opened my mouth to say something, but didn't get a chance as Nate continued his exploration. He licked against my teeth and then the tip of his tongue touched mine. I jerked back at first, shocked, but when he followed me, playing with me, I couldn't help but play a little bit, too. My whole body was tingling. I didn't want him to stop.

One of Nate's legs slid over mine, his knee resting on the bed between my knees. I wasn't sure, but thought I could feel his engorged private part pressing against my thigh.

I longed to touch him there.

And while I was busy thinking about that, his lips left mine. I would have protested, but he was trailing kisses along my neck, sending the most appealing sensations all through my body. I lifted my chin, and actually groaned out loud when his mouth found the curve between my neck and my shoulder. I had no idea it felt so good to be touched there. Glorying in the sensation, not wanting to miss any part of it, it took me several seconds to realize where Nate's tongue would be going next.

When I figured it out, I panicked, pulling his head back up to kiss me again. He didn't seem to mind, his kisses as avid as they'd been moments before and I got lost in them, in the feelings they aroused.

My nipples ached and I wasn't sure what to do about that. When I could stand it no longer, I arched, pressing my breasts against Nate's chest. He understood things I didn't and before I knew what was happening, his hand was over my breast, kneading it, alleviating some of the almost painful tension.

I was shocked by my moans of pleasure, but couldn't hold them back. First one and then the other, he fondled my breasts, sending delicious shivers all over my body, saying nothing. I was thankful for that. I didn't have to think, to be accountable or embarrassed. I could just float on this wave of sensation.

I'd been squirming around so much, my dress was twisted up around my bottom. I thought Nate was going to straighten it when he sat me up. Instead, I felt the zipper slide down, exposing my back to the cool night air.

"Do you mind?" he asked, his voice husky, almost unrecognizable.

I shook my head. I wasn't surprised when I felt the catch on my bra give way.

Nor did I particularly care when the front of my dress fell forward at a gentle tug from his fingers. I allowed him to slide my bra down my arms and reveal breasts that, until then, had only been seen by my doctor and me.

"They're so incredibly beautiful," he whispered, staring down at them.

"Kiss me?" It might bother me later that I was being so bold, but it sure didn't then.

He leaned forward and I closed my eyes, waiting for the touch of his lips against mine, and jerked when his tongue flicked across my nipple instead.

"Oh!"

Pushing me back against the pillows, he closed his mouth over me, and my pelvis started to rock.

"You like it?" he asked, his teeth lightly grazing me.

"Mmm-hmm."

Nate did things to me I'd never read about, aroused indescribable sensations that had me begging for more until I didn't recognize myself at all in the woman lying on that soft mattress, dress down around my hips.

"I want to make love to you."

Instead of instilling the fear I would have expected, Nate's words spurred me on.

"I want that, too."

He stopped—everything. Raising himself above me, he peered right into my eyes. "You sure?"

Grabbing his neck, I pulled him back down. "I am—as long as you keep doing what you're doing."

With a groan and a chuckle, Nate lowered himself, sliding his arms beneath me to hug me tight. "The second you want me to stop, you tell me." His words, whispered against my ear, sent chills down my body.

"Okay."

"Promise?"

"Mmm-hmm." Didn't he know I'd promise him anything right then?

Kissing his way down my body, removing my clothes as he went, Nate kept my mind too occupied to think, to allow panic to take hold. I felt a second of doubt when he stood and stepped out of his clothes, when I saw the swollen part of him that had been beneath that zipper.

But before I could give voice to the fears distracting me, Nate was back.

His hands worked magic and his tongue seemed to be everywhere. I sucked in a breath when I felt his velvet-covered hardness between my legs.

"It's going to hurt for a second." Nate's voice was strained as he suspended himself above me. "There's nothing I can do about that."

I nodded, waiting, needing him more than I feared what was to come.

I cried out when Nate surged forward. Nothing could have prepared me for that initial shock, but as he filled me and gently started to move, I ignored the burning and concentrated on the sensation he was generating.

And somehow, miraculously, the buzzing returned, grew, until I was moving as fiercely as he was, taking him as much as he was taking me. It was as though my body had been possessed. I had to have him. Had to climb. Had to get someplace I'd never been before.

And when I arrived, just seconds before Nate spilled

himself inside me, I knew that nothing I'd read about bliss could ever compare to this. I'd reached heaven long before I'd expected to.

Chapter 6

Almost one year to the day I'd married Nate, in the summer of 1969, astronaut Neil Armstrong set foot on the moon, the first man to ever do so. And I went into labor—feeling like the first woman to ever experience anything so exhilarating and excruciating at the same time. Nate was home, thank goodness, in between summer camp sessions, and was calm and reassuring as he collected the bag I'd packed a month before and carried us both out to the station wagon we'd bought the previous winter when we'd found out I was pregnant.

I could barely sit up in the car and almost passed out when the next pain came. "I…can't." I heard my voice from far away.

I'd never missed the convent—the church—as much as I did at that moment.

"Yes, you can, Liza." It wasn't the firmness in Nate's voice that brought me back. It was the fear.

"Breathe," he said, panting and huffing like we'd learned in the class Nate had insisted we attend.

I tried. I really did. But the pain was so intense I couldn't concentrate.

The turn signal was the first sound I heard as the pain subsided. I focused on that long enough to get through the rest of the contraction.

"Obviously Dr. Lamaze has never been in labor," I muttered, eyes closed as I slumped against the seat. "He has no idea how much that hurts if he thinks a little breathing and relaxing is enough to distract you from it."

"Women have been flocking to his classes for the last ten years," Nate said. As soon as he'd learned we were having a baby, he'd insisted we both read everything there was to find about childbirth. "I was hoping that meant he'd found a way to make this easier for you."

"My mom had a shot, went to sleep and woke up skinny again." As ready as I was to have this baby, to finally hold my little son or daughter in my arms, I was scared to death about what the next few hours might bring.

Even with modern medicine, women still died in childbirth. I couldn't bear the idea of leaving Nate.

Or our child.

Still, that didn't give me any excuse to lash out. "I'm sorry. I don't know why I'm being so cranky."

"Be as cranky as you need to be, honey," Nate said.

We were stopped at a light and I opened my eyes to see him smiling over at me. I smiled back, and soon we were accelerating again.

Please, God, I'll suffer gladly if you'll just get me and the baby through this okay.

"It's a boy!"

The doctor's voice brought me out of the pain-induced fog I'd fallen into even before reaching the hospital in Denver.

"A boy?" I asked, leaning forward in an attempt to see. "Are you sure?"

The tent of sheets around my lower body prevented me from getting little more than a glimpse—of Nate. Moving in as close to the doctor as he could get, he glanced down, then up at me, his face bearing a huge grin.

"Yep, it's a boy."

"Would you like to cut the cord?"

The doctor's question fell on deaf ears as my strong and oh-so-capable husband slid to the floor—grabbed by the nurse who, thankfully, helped break his fall. He'd been so busy breathing with me, he'd hyperventilated.

Because I was going to be breast-feeding I couldn't take much for my discomfort, but managed to sleep anyway once I was settled in my semiprivate but as yet unshared room. Keith Armstrong Grady—named after

Nate's little brother and the astronaut who'd also mani-fested a miracle that day—was in the nursery until feeding time.

I dreamed heavily, although I couldn't remember about what. I only knew I was feeling particularly emo-tional as I slowly regained consciousness. The antisep-tic smell reminded me where I was before I was fully awake. And then my eyes flew open—looking for the portable bassinet that was supposed to appear beside my bed.

Had I slept through feeding time?

The room was empty. Or so I thought. Until I saw the woman sitting in a chair beside the bed, watching me.

"Mama?"

Tears welled in her eyes as she nodded. She'd gained some new wrinkles around her eyes over the many months since I'd seen her. "I'm sorry I let you down, baby. I should've been here, seeing you through all these firsts."

"Is everything okay?" Was she there to tell me some-thing awful? Why else would she end the year-and-a-half-long silence between us?

"Yes," she said, approaching my bed, not much heavier than she'd been when I was young. She was wearing a light-colored shift that I didn't recognize, but as she smiled—a reassuring expression I'd seen many times growing up—my heart filled with peace. "I've seen Keith and he's just perfect, Eliza. Nate's with him now. And William and your sisters, too. We all came as soon as he called."

Nate had called my family?

"He's a good man, Eliza. He loves you. And I should have trusted you enough to know that."

I would've thought I was still dreaming except that my lower body felt like it was on fire.

"Is Daddy here?"

Mom's face sobered and she shook her head. "But give him time. He'll come around."

I nodded, smiled and reached up to give my mother a hug, trying to stem the hurt caused by my father's absence. Dad could have whatever time he needed. I had a husband who adored me, a son with ten fingers and ten toes, a family who'd come to be by my side. I could afford to be generous.

The first time I held Keith to my breast I knew I would have been incomplete had I chosen to stay in the convent my whole life. The baby's suckling satisfied me in a way I hadn't known was possible. I was meant to be a mother.

"I love you, Eliza." Nate's voice was full of awe as he watched me feed our son. Mom and the others had left for the evening, going back to our house to ready it for my homecoming.

"I love you, too," I told my husband. "More than you'll ever know." I might be his third wife, but I was the first—and only—woman to have his child.

Nate held out a finger to the baby, sliding it beneath the tightly clenched hand. The sight of that thick, masculine finger so tenderly touching our newborn son brought tears to my eyes.

"He's so tiny."

Choked up, I nodded.

"Thank you."

I glanced at him then. "For what?"

Nate nodded toward the baby. "Him. Marrying me. All of it. You gave up so much."

Raising a hand to Nate's head, I ran my fingers through his hair, loving the familiar feel of the silky strands against my skin. "I gave up nothing compared to what I've gained in return, Nate Grady. I'm the one who should be grateful."

Keith was only a couple of months old when I feared our ideal life was coming to an end. The morning started out innocuously enough. I'd been telling Nate that I'd heard there'd been an Elvis Presley convention and 2500 people had attended. I couldn't believe so many people would give up an entire weekend just to gather with strangers who liked the same songs they did.

"That reminds me," Nate had said, somewhat distracted as he poured himself a bowl of cereal while I sat at the table with Keith at my breast. "There's a hotel management convention in Hawaii next month. Walt wants me to go."

My heart fell. Hawaii was half a world away. Or at least it felt like it.

"Can't someone else go?"

"It's a managers' convention. I'm the manager," Nate said, taking a spoonful of cereal on his way to the table. "Besides, it's an honor. I want to go. I've never been to Hawaii."

I wasn't going to be a clingy wife. Or give him a chance to tell me I was acting immature—not that Nate had ever once accused me of that.

I wasn't going to hold him back.

"Okay," I said, proud of myself for being able to say that—and mean it. "But we'll miss you."

His spoon hung suspended between his mouth and the bowl. "We?"

"Keith and I."

"You're going with me!" He frowned. "Your mom offered to come and babysit anytime."

"I can't go," I said, glad at least that he'd wanted me to. "I'm breast-feeding, remember?"

"He'll be three months old by then. You can wean him."

"No, I can't." We'd been through all of this before the baby was born—had a solid plan that we both felt good about. "Breast-fed babies are generally healthier," I reminded him. "We said I'd feed him until he's six months old and past all the newborn baby dangers."

"That was before we knew we'd have a once-in-a-lifetime chance to spend a week in Hawaii, all expenses paid."

A week? "Nate!" Keith whimpered and I resettled

him. "Even if I wasn't breast-feeding, I wouldn't want to leave him for an entire week. He's only two months old! Anything could happen. This is a critical time in a baby's life. He needs his mother."

"But you don't mind leaving me for a week." The surly tone of voice was so unlike Nate.

Come to think of it, my husband had been acting a little out of sorts for a while now. I'd been so consumed with first-time motherhood and worrying about getting it right that I'd somehow lost touch with Nate.

"I'm not the one leaving," I told him gently.

"You mean it." He stared at me. "You really won't come."

"Not without Keith."

"You'd choose him over me."

"Nate!" I frowned, getting kind of scared. "Don't be ridiculous! This isn't a contest. Keith is yours as much as he's mine."

He stood up, taking his half-eaten bowl of cereal over to the garbage. "All I know is that since you had that baby, you've been out of our bed more than in it. When I call from work, you're always distracted. I can't remember the last time you asked me how my day went. And now you're turning down a chance for a trip to paradise with me."

Sick to my stomach, I sat there feeling far too exposed as I fed my son—and utterly helpless, as well. Since Keith's birth, I'd been too tired even to read the dog-eared copy of *Jane Eyre* on my nightstand, let alone tend to an energetic and active husband.

I'd been too consumed with my own joy and the responsibilities of a new mother to think much about the man I loved. Nate might be acting out of character today, but as far as he was concerned, I'd been doing exactly the same thing since the first day I'd held our baby in my arms.

"I'll try to do better" was all I could think to say. While I thought Nate was wrong to expect me to leave the baby for an entire week when he was still so young, I knew I'd treated Nate poorly, too. At best, I'd taken him for granted. At worst, I'd ignored him. "I have no excuse except to say I was just trying to be a good mother."

"I don't *want* you to have to try to do better," Nate said, grabbing his keys and windbreaker with the resort logo. "That's the thing, Eliza. You used to care enough about me that you didn't have to try. It just happened."

He walked out before I could reply.

Moving the baby to my other breast, I sat stunned. I felt as though I'd been slapped.

That night, when Nate got home, Keith was already fed and bathed, and he'd been down for at least four hours. I'd bathed, as well, styling my hair and even applying a little of the makeup Walt's daughter, Mary, had helped me buy and learn how to wear. I had steaks on the broiler, a glass of wine poured for Nate, and was wearing the negligee he'd bought me for our first anniversary.

A gown I hadn't yet had an occasion to wear.

Nate had called that afternoon. He'd apologized. I had, too, although he'd said there was no need. He'd confessed his shame at finding that he'd been jealous of his own son. He'd said I was a great mom and he was eternally grateful.

Nate hadn't mentioned it, but I suspected part of his problem was the fact we hadn't made love in almost four months. I hadn't really noticed the time passing—or felt particularly sexy—as my body ballooned with the baby and then recovered from what felt like a million stitches. But I'd been starting to feel the urge lately, and if it was this noticeable to me, the wait had to be equally difficult for him.

Twenty minutes before I expected him home, I heard the piano and, spraying on his favorite perfume, went quickly downstairs to the dining room, which was home solely to the scarred old piano he'd had since childhood.

His back was to the door and he didn't know I was there. I started toward him, intending to put my arms around him when he began to sing. "My Cup Runneth Over."

The first line of the song stopped me in my tracks and tears filled my eyes.

We were going to be okay.

Or so I thought. Less than a week later, Nate and I were in bed, in the throes of lovemaking, when the baby began to cry.

"Leave him for just a second," my husband said, his voice strained and out of breath.

I tried. Thinking of the man I loved, I opened to him, welcomed him, but as the baby's cries grew louder, I couldn't focus, couldn't do anything but lie there like a rag doll.

"Forget it."

Before I knew what was happening, Nate had rolled off me and off our bed—without an orgasm. A moment later, Keith's cries stopped. I didn't move, worried about Nate's mood, afraid I'd hurt his feelings. I could tell by the sounds from the nursery that he was changing the baby.

He brought Keith to me. "Here's your mama," he said gently, settling the baby against me, and my heart soared for an instant.

Until, instead of joining us, Nate left the room. I heard his feet on the stairs. The clang of his keys. And the front door closing.

Tears rolled slowly down my cheeks the entire time our son nursed.

Nate never came back to bed that night.

"Where were you?" Those were the first words out of my mouth when, at five o'clock the next morning, Nate came through the back door just as I finished feeding Keith at the kitchen table.

"Out."

"I realize that. Out where?" I could understand and forgive a lot of things. One I would not. Ever.

If Nate had found his welcome in another woman's body…

"Driving." He dropped his keys on the counter. Went to make a pot of coffee—decaffeinated because I was breast-feeding.

"Alone?"

"Of course."

"All night?"

Nate didn't turn around, didn't deny the validity of my obvious suspicion.

"Yes."

Neither would he out-and-out lie to me. I knew that without a doubt.

"You told me once that you'd inevitably do some things that would disappoint me. You said I'd do them, too."

He stood at the counter in front of a pot that was starting to percolate.

"I just want it understood, Nate Grady, that disappointment I can handle, but if you ever step out on me, if you ever touch another woman or let her touch you, I will surely die."

Swinging around slowly, he gave me a long, hard stare. And then, still without saying a word, he left the room.

Five minutes later, from upstairs in my bathroom where I was covering my sobs with the sound of the shower, I could hear the piano. Nate started out slowly, with a soft, sad-sounding piece. He was hurting as much as I was. Maybe more.

Because I had Keith's unconditional love staring me in the face all day, every day, while Nate went out in the world to provide for us. And when he came home at night, I was the one Keith reached for when he was hungry or in need. That had to make Nate feel excluded.

Once it had been Nate and me against the world. Now it was Keith and me, with Nate on the outside looking in.

I could see it happening. I just didn't know what to do about it. My baby was helpless.

Nate was not.

I adjusted Keith's feeding schedule. It took a few days but I arranged it so that the baby was still up for a couple of hours when Nate got home. That way he had more time with his son.

And he and I had more uninterrupted time late at night. It seemed odd, keeping a baby up so late, but anything that might help heal the rift between us was worth a try.

On the fourth night, he was playing the piano as I fed the baby and put him to bed. This was already becoming a routine. One that I loved. I'd moved my rocking chair from the living room to the dining room and sat beside the piano while Keith nursed and fell asleep—listening to his father play.

I smiled as I came downstairs after putting Keith in his crib—to Nate's rowdy rendition of "Great Balls of Fire." He always played that when he was feeling aroused. On a whim, I unbuttoned my shirt as I walked, and unclipped my bra. Leaving a trail of clothing behind me, I entered the dining room topless—something I wouldn't be able to get away with these days if the baby hadn't just nursed.

Something I'd never even *thought* of doing before.

Glancing up as I sauntered in, Nate missed a key. I grinned. And went for the button on my jeans. Seeing that I had my husband's complete attention I shimmied to get out of them and left them in a pile on the shiny wood floor. Dressed only in a pair of panties Nate had bought me, I climbed up onto the piano bench and hitched myself up to sit on the scarred wood of the instrument Nate was still attempting to play, my feet dangling above the keys.

"You're asking for trouble, woman," he growled playfully.

"I'm looking for trouble, sir."

Nate didn't let me down. I'd never made love on a piano bench before. Never done it sitting on a man's lap, either.

That night I did both.

And loved every second of it.

Chapter 7

Our second son, Jimmy, named after my father, who still wouldn't acknowledge me, was born just thirteen months after Keith. With two boys in diapers, one of them walking and refusing most naps, I was busy from morning until night, but I'd grown a lot more comfortable with motherhood—and had mastered the fine art of juggling many roles at once. I could clean up vomit, vacuum and cook almost simultaneously. And still smell good and have a smile on my face when my husband got home.

The smile wasn't hard. After more than two years of marriage, I adored my husband as much as ever. Every night, no matter how tired he might be, Nate played with his sons, bathed them and then serenaded them to sleep.

I still felt pangs when I drove by the Catholic church on the next block. I'd pulled into the parking lot a few times during mass, just to sit there and feel…close. But even then, I didn't regret marrying Nate.

And life went on.

Singer Elton John made his first United States appearance when Jimmy was two weeks old, and Nate, who had a hankering for his songs, celebrated by taking us out for a night on the town. We took the boys—Keith, really, as Jimmy was breast-feeding—to Denver for his first fast-food hamburger.

He didn't want anything to do with the mustard-smeared offering, but he loved French fries and begged to have them with every meal after that.

My mother came to stay with us the fall after Jimmy was born. She was a great help to me as I adjusted to dealing with an overactive toddler and a newborn. And it took very little time for her and Nate to solidify the bond they'd tentatively formed during my mother's brief visit after Keith's birth. One night at the piano and she was hooked.

Mom stayed for nearly a month and it soon became clear that we were going to need a bigger house. Three bedrooms wasn't enough anymore. Mom and I looked for three days until we found the perfect place. A log home close to the mountains.

Nate loved it on sight and within six weeks, we'd moved in.

William, June, Alice and Bonnie took turns visiting that year, as well. June had moved back to California, and my sisters came together, without their families. I missed my nieces and nephews and Nate promised that next summer we'd make it home for a visit of our own.

William still wasn't married. At my instigation, Nate tried his best to hook him up, but William wasn't having any of it. He said he had a list of things to do before he planned to settle down. And when Nate started in on him, he said, "Hey, big brother, I seem to remember you were pushing what—thirty-four, wasn't it?—when you married my sister."

By that standard, William, at twenty-seven, had some time.

With a son on each hip, Nate didn't say another word.

We didn't make it home that summer, after all. I was pregnant again—due in October. That would make three babies in just over three years. I wondered if I was going to have another boy. While I secretly longed for a little girl, I knew it would be more practical to have a son. I had all the clothes and toys already.

Nate's job was going well. The resort had grown so much, Walt was talking about expanding into Utah and possibly Nevada. He sent Nate to scout out some sites in Tahoe. Nate wanted me to come and I called my mother immediately, hoping she could stay with the boys.

She flew out the next weekend and seven months pregnant, I went on a romantic getaway with my husband. We were only gone four days, but they were days I'd remember for the rest of my life. I'd forgotten how observant Nate was, how attuned to everything around him. I'd forgotten how marvelous it felt to be the sole recipient of his attention. But the one thing I hadn't forgotten was how much I loved him.

On the day Sarah Elizabeth Grady was born, Disney-world opened in Orlando, Florida. I knew this was an omen of the magic our little girl was going to bring to my life. I finally had a daughter.

Nate couldn't have been more thrilled. He called at least four times a day to ask how Sarah was doing and always went to her the second he got home at night. If I hadn't been so happy, I might've been a bit jealous that our daughter got his first kiss at the end of the day, but I couldn't find it in me to do more than grin and wait my turn.

Life was hectic. Keith was potty training, Jimmy walking. I was breast-feeding again. And the house didn't get cleaned as often. I couldn't make myself care about that. I kept the floors sanitary, the laundry done and managed to cook healthy meals. The rest didn't seem to matter.

I invited my parents for Christmas that year. My mother came alone—two days after the holiday. I was beginning to understand that my father was never going to

forgive me. He thought I'd disrespected his greater experience and knowledge. He thought I'd dishonored him.
I had a recurring dream in which he'd show up on my
doorstep with presents for all three kids. The dream eased
the constant ache I felt because of the hole in my heart.
In a strange way it gave me hope.

And, according to Mom, he still believed Nate was
going to hurt me. He didn't seem to realize that *he* was
the only man in my life who'd done that.

Two days after Mom left, on the second of January,
1972, Sarah Elizabeth Grady died in her sleep. Crib
death, they called it.

I called it cruel. Unfair. Impossible.

"No, Nate, she's *not* dead," I told Sarah's father as he
pried my hands away from the tiny casket someone had
chosen and mistakenly placed my tiny daughter in.

"Come on, Liza, we have to go."

The visitation had been over for almost an hour. My
mother had long since taken the boys home to bed.

"I'm not leaving her."

"I'm sorry, baby, you have to." His words were little
more than a whisper as he bent over me where I half lay
against the small pine box.

"I can't." While my spirit was slowly crumbling, my
voice remained strong.

"Yes, you can." I had a flash of memory—Nate saying
those same words to me in that same tone. The day he'd
driven me to the hospital to deliver our first child.

Forever ago.

He'd been right then. I could do it. I had. And repeated the experience twice more.

But this time he was dead wrong.

Dead, dead wrong.

As dead wrong as that precious little body lying so stiffly just inches from my face.

As dead as I wanted to be.

Sarah's sweet, chubby cheeks blurred as my eyes welled with tears.

"I can't, Nate." My voice broke and my body shook with sobs that hurt my bones. "I just can't do it." I heard my wails, wondered in some obscure part of my brain what the mortician must think of me, but didn't have the strength to give a damn.

Nate stood beside me, holding me up as I held on to the silky fabric lining our baby's casket, crying with me. I could feel his tears dropping on the back of my neck and knew he was grieving, too.

The weight of his pain was too much to bear.

I'd done this. To Sarah. To Nate.

This was my penance. The price I guess I'd always known I would someday pay.

This was God's way of punishing me for breaking my word to Him. I should never have left the convent.

This was my fault.

I begged God to have enough mercy to take me home.

My chest was soaked. I felt something sticky on my breasts. Pulling myself up out of a deep sleep I knew I didn't want to leave, I thought of Sarah, hungry, needing to eat, and opened my eyes.

And then closed them again. Remembering.

The setting sun was shining in on me. I could feel its warmth on my face.

It was afternoon and I was in bed.

I didn't care. Another drop of milk slid down the side of my breast to the mattress beneath me. The thick protective pads I wore inside my bra were drenched, heavy with unused milk.

There were no tears left to cry, just this weighty sadness that infiltrated my bones and pinned me to the bed.

"How long's she been asleep?" Nate's voice. Home from work.

"More than an hour." Mama was there, too. In the room. They were probably staring at me. I didn't have to feign sleep. I was comatose whether I was conscious or not. "I'm worried sick about her, Nate. I told James I'd be home by the end of the week, but I can't leave her. Or the boys."

The boys. My sons. They deserved better than me. I wasn't good enough to earn the honor of raising Sarah. Would I harm them, too?

And James, my father. He knew about me. I didn't blame him for staying away all these years. Even the death of my precious little Sarah hadn't been enough to bring him back.

"I think you should go." Nate's voice sounded tired.

He needed a woman who was worthy of him.

"Who'll watch over her? And the boys? She's barely twenty-three, Nate. Still a baby herself. Too young to handle…this…and two small boys. I can't leave her."

"She's been in bed for a week. Refusing to take the medication her doctor gave her to dry up her milk and to help with depression. We can't continue this way."

Was he ready to dump me then? I couldn't blame him.

"I don't know what else to do…" Mama sounded like she was going to cry.

I was responsible for that, too. If I hadn't been so numb, I'd have hated myself.

"We're not helping her, Mom. As long as you're here, she doesn't have to *do* anything."

"You think if I go she's just going to get up and be fine?"

"I think she has two sons to take care of and if no one else is here to do it, she'll have to."

Dear Nate. He still thought a person was in control of her own life, that we actually had choices and our own inner strength would see us through. I used to believe that, too.

Not anymore.

"I'll call the airline after dinner, but, Nate, you have to promise me you'll call if she gets into any trouble…."

Mama didn't mean breaking laws kind of trouble; I knew that. She was afraid I was going to kill myself.

I wasn't afraid of that. I was thinking about it, though.

I got up when Mama left the next day. Waved goodbye to her and Nate. He was going to work after dropping her at the airport. It was mid-January, busy season for him. And too cold for the boys to play outside. I brought toys to the living room, put up the gates, brought in a box of graham crackers, turned on the television set and lay down on the couch. I didn't move—except for one trek to the kitchen, some diaper changes for Jimmy and a couple of trips to the potty with Keith. I was still there when Nate got home.

"Why didn't you turn on any lights?"

I hadn't noticed. "We didn't need them."

Jimmy and Keith were both asleep, lying on pillows in front of the television.

"What's for dinner?"

I had no idea. I stared at him blankly.

"Eliza, you still have two healthy, growing children. They have to eat."

"They had graham crackers."

"That's all they've had all day?"

"No." I frowned. Tried to be who he wanted me to be. "They had fruit, mixed vegetables and chicken and rice for lunch."

"You fed Keith out of baby food jars?"

"He likes it."

"He's three years old."

I had no reply to that. Nor to Nate's repeated attempts to rouse me enough to make dinner. It's not that I didn't want them all to eat. I did. But I didn't have the energy or the focus to prepare even the simplest meal.

The thought of going through the cupboards to find out what was there made me dizzy. Nauseous.

Jimmy was still eating baby food, anyway. And Keith wouldn't mind it again. That just left Nate.

In the end, he went out for hamburgers, taking the boys with him.

I woke up when Nate crawled into bed beside me that night. Lying silently, waiting for him to settle with his back to me, listening for the relaxed breathing that would tell me he was asleep, I felt consumed by guilt. I'd let him down so completely.

Let them all down.

The mattress shifted, dipped close to my side.

"Liza? You awake?"

If I hadn't been, I would be now. Nate was sliding his arm beneath me, pulling me against him.

He was so warm. I wanted to be held. And yet I was too cold to ever recover. I lay there, limp, letting him touch me, aware that his fingers were running lightly along my neck, but feeling nothing.

"Come on, baby. No one else can do this for you. It's up to you."

That's what he didn't understand. I was powerless.

He kissed me then. A soft, tender caress that would have broken my heart with its sweetness if I'd had a heart left to break.

"Kiss me, love." His tongue swept over mine, coaxing lips that were lifeless. "Let yourself *feel*."

He thought I had control, that I could somehow make the numbness go away.

When his hand moved to my breast, when my nipple quivered at his touch, I turned my back to him.

Nate Grady was the temptation that had started me down this long road to hell—lured me from the life that would have protected me—and given me the sweet little spirits I'd inadvertently hurt with my weakness.

Did Nate know that Sarah's death was my fault? My penance?

Did he secretly hate me?

I'd thought about Sister Michael Damien that day. I'd written to the sisters a few times after I left St. Catherine's. Sent them pictures of the boys when they were born, but I'd never heard back.

All I could see now was the concerned look on Sister Damien's face the day I'd told her Nate was divorced—the day she knew I'd be leaving not only the convent, but the Church.

"I'm not going to quit, Eliza." His voice was loud and clear in the darkness of our bedroom. Resolute. "We're a team, you and I. Part of the same whole. As long as it takes, I'm going to be here."

With that, he rolled over, his back to me, and went to sleep.

I lay awake listening to him breathe—wishing I could find the escape of unconsciousness that had carried me through until that day—while tears dripped slowly down to wet my pillow.

★ ★ ★

I couldn't get up the next morning. I honestly tried. Nate cajoled. He brought the boys in, put them on the bed with me. I just couldn't do it. Filled with self-loathing, I was paralyzed with the fear of what I might bring to any day I entered.

A part of me knew I was in trouble. That I should get help. But I couldn't bridge the gap inside me that would take me from realization to action. I could find no solace in my faith, in the Bible verses I knew by heart or even my precious *Jane Eyre*.

Nate took the boys to work with him. I spent the day staring at the darkness in my mind.

"Okay, that's it!"

I jerked awake as the covers were torn from my body.

"Look at you! You haven't been up all day, have you?"

I could count on one hand the times my husband had screamed at me. I stared at him.

"Get up, Eliza." His voice was louder. "I mean it!"

Nate didn't get angry. Not like this.

"Now!"

His grip was not gentle as he yanked me into a sitting position. My legs wouldn't move, but that didn't stop him. Nate hauled me up, over his shoulder, carried me into the bathroom. My head hung down as he bent to turn on the shower and then I came upright again as he stood me inside, gown and all.

"The boys are in their high chairs, having juice while

they wait for dinner. You have five minutes to get washed and out of this shower. Another five to dress, and then you'll come down to the kitchen and make dinner for your family. Is that clear?"

He was no longer yelling at me. This new, softer tone was more menacing.

Blinking at him through the water spraying down on my head, I did the only thing I could do. I nodded.

I managed cereal and toast with peanut butter and jelly. Nate pretended to busy himself with a leak under the kitchen sink, but I could see him watching every move I made. If I lived through this horrible time, I would never forget that moment.

As pathetic and damaging as I was, the man loved me. I had some value.

"One of the front-desk clerks quit today," he said as he ate cold cereal on a snowy January night without so much as raising his eyebrows. "Starting tomorrow, you're coming to work with me. You can help out at the front desk."

I couldn't do that. "What about the boys?"

"For now, they can play in my office. There's a sleeping room that has a couple of port-a-cribs close by that we can use for naps. And they can attend the guest day care facility the rest of the time."

"I can't, Nate."

"You can and you will."

"You can't make me."

His eyes were steely as they met mine. "Watch me."

Chapter 8

I screwed up at the front desk. Reservations were lost. I gave someone the wrong key to a room. Messages weren't relayed. None of it was on purpose; I just couldn't focus.

"See, I told you," I said to Nate when, after the fourth incident, he called me into his office.

His scrutiny made me uncomfortable and I tried not to fidget. The boys were playing with a plastic train set, spitting as they made engine sounds. They'd be turning two and three this summer. I wondered if Mama would come and throw them a party.

"I'm short a housekeeper." Nate's voice brought me back. "See Maria on the seventh floor and she'll set you up."

"I have to clean rooms?"

"You got any better ideas?" His look challenged me to argue with him. "Like maybe an institution where you can sit and be a vegetable for the rest of your life? Or drugs that'll keep you numb?"

He was scaring me.

Had I been more myself, I would've known that was a good sign.

"I hate you, Nate Grady." I wasn't sure I meant the words, but in that second, I felt them.

"And I love you."

His reply made me feel like a pile of dirt. With one last look at my sons, I left the room.

"I want a vacation."

"Sorry."

I stomped my foot where I stood in front of my husband's desk, an action that had little effect on the plush piled carpet. "Nate, I've been working for no pay for six weeks. I want some time off."

He didn't glance up from the papers he was perusing. "In case you hadn't noticed, it's the busy season around here. No one gets time off."

"Then hire someone to take my place."

He peered up at me long enough to make me squirm. "What time did you get up on Saturday?"

So I'd had a relapse. "Nate." I put all the anger building up inside me into saying his name.

He had the audacity to grin at me. "That's right, Liza, get mad. Yell, scream, hit something."

I wasn't like that. Didn't do those things.

Without another word I went back to work.

"I miss my sons," I said.

"I miss my wife."

Nate and I hadn't made love since Sarah died.

"Why are you still so good to me?"

"I love you."

My heart welled with so much feeling it almost suffocated me.

The boys were in bed and we were sitting over a last cup of coffee at the kitchen table one night in mid-May. There'd been an assassination attempt on Alabama's governor, George Wallace, that day, which left him paralyzed. The man hadn't abandoned a convent calling and yet a bad thing had happened to him. Martin Luther King had been serving God and the public with his life when he'd been killed.

"Sarah didn't die because I'm a bad person." I spoke the words out loud, but was really talking to myself.

"No, she didn't."

"I'm scared, Nate." There. I'd admitted it. "I'm starting to feel again and I'm afraid the pain's going to be too intense."

"There are times it seems that way. But they pass."

I reached for his hand, holding it between both of mine on the table. "You hurt, too."

"Yeah."

"And I haven't been there to give you any comfort at all."

"You lie in bed beside me every night, Liza. You breathe. You get up in the morning and force yourself to do work you don't want to do. You love our sons. You miss them. Every single one of these things comforts me."

"I've been selfish."

"You've been surviving. Sarah's death devastated you."

"Why didn't it you?" The question wasn't accusation. Just the opposite. I wanted to know how he did it. How he kept going in the face of such impossible agony.

"I have a life outside of home." His words surprised me. "I was able to leave here and go someplace where I'm someone else. The boss. Not Daddy. Not husband. Those times offered me a break from the constant hurting."

He squeezed my hand. "Your life was all here, completely involved with being a mother. And suddenly, being a mother was the most painful experience you'd ever had to endure. You had no escape."

I now understood why he'd forced me to go to work.

"You make me sound a lot more noble than I feel."

"You're human, Liza."

And with that came good and bad. Pain and joy.

"Will you do something for me?"

"Of course."

"Will you play the piano?"

He hadn't touched a key since Sarah's death. The drawn look on his face told me he wasn't going to now.

"Please?"

"The boys are asleep."

"Until four months ago, they fell asleep to the piano every night."

He was still going to refuse.

"I'm cleaning toilets, Nate." Making myself recover.

His chin dropped to his chest.

I stood, yanked on his hand. "Come on, I'll sit with you."

He let me pull him into the other room and sat down when I slid the bench out. And, hands resting limply in his lap, he stared at the keys.

"Let's do chopsticks," I said, grasping at straws. It was the only thing I knew how to play.

With two fingers I started softly and then grew louder, pounding the keys. Harder and harder. Until my fingers hurt. I didn't even know I was crying until tears plopped down on the ivory slats.

Before I could stop myself, I was pounding out horrible, discordant sounds, my fists slamming down on the instrument with everything I had. I could feel the edges of the keys scraping my knuckles and I didn't care.

We'd lost so much. Too much. Our precious daughter. Our joy. Even this. The special beauty that Nate had brought into our home.

I was angry. So angry.

And then, in the midst of the cacophony, came a single, true note. Followed by another. My hands stilled as I looked at the strong fingers moving shakily over the keys.

I wasn't sure Nate was playing a song. Or if he was actually aware of what he was doing. But slowly, a tune surfaced, and for the first time in four months my heart knew a moment of peace.

Somehow, through all the noise, he'd found "My Cup Runneth Over." I felt again the way I'd felt the very first time I'd heard that song. And subsequent memories surfaced, as well.

Nate didn't play long. Half an hour, maybe. But it was enough. He'd be back at the piano again. Soon.

We climbed the stairs to our room together, stopping, as if by unspoken agreement, to look in on the boys. Both of our sons were sleeping soundly, Jimmy with his diapered butt in the air as always and Keith with two fingers in his mouth.

And that night, we made a different kind of love. Slow. Lingering. And the completion, when it came, left me languid, relaxed, ready to fall asleep in my husband's arms.

We were blessed.

Very blessed.

Times were changing. In 1972 the largest scandal ever to hit the White House was exposed by a security guard who noticed a piece of adhesive tape on a door that left it unlocked, allowing five men to steal key Democratic documents. By January 1975, at least six government officials had been found guilty in the Watergate conspiracy and were sentenced to thirty years in prison. Also early in that year, *The Jeffersons,* the first successful black sitcom, premiered on primetime television. And Pennsylvania was the first state to allow girls to compete with boys.

Sometimes it seemed like every day there'd be another radical change, and I lived those years with some uneasiness, but I learned how to be flexible. In September of 1975, Jimmy started kindergarten, leaving his mama at loose ends. But Sarah's death had taught me what I needed to do. With my out-of-date California teaching degree in hand, I enrolled in classes to earn a current Colorado certification.

I had no plans to work full-time; I was first and foremost a wife and mother. I just had to keep my mind focused on other things. Positive things. I was room mother for both of my boys that year, joined the PTA, got involved with T-ball. And through the university, I volunteered at a battered women's shelter in Denver one morning a month.

I wrote to my father several times during those years—always with the same result. Nothing. No response. And I continued to have dreams in which he showed up at my door, always bringing gifts for my children. Once I even dreamed I was sitting at mass and he slid into the pew beside me.

Nate was traveling a lot. Walt sold the resort to a well-known international chain and with travel getting easier, more resorts were popping up around the globe. Nate, who'd been let go after the buy-out, started his own business as an independent consultant on the building and start-up of several resorts in California and Nevada and soon had more jobs than he could handle. He loved the work. We loved the financial freedom it afforded us. He was enjoying the opportunity to spend some time with his brother, Keith's, buddy Arnold. But he was often gone and the boys and I missed him terribly.

Shortly after Halloween of 1975, I noticed that Keith and Jimmy were squabbling a lot. At first I put the unusual dissension down to sugar overload and threw away the rest of their candy stash. But as the arguments escalated to the point where I had to separate them on an almost daily basis, and they both started talking back to me in spite of the punishments I handed out, I began to wonder if the problem was a lack of male influence in the household.

I told Nate about my concerns when he called one night and I could hear the frustration in his voice because he couldn't be home with us, helping more. But I also heard laughing in the background and the resentment I'd begun to feel was a little more difficult to fight.

He promised to call the boys the next day. They seemed calmer after that. Until Saturday. I don't know who started it, but while I was cleaning the boys' bathroom, I suddenly heard screaming and slapping, and before I could get to Keith's bedroom, I heard a sickening thud, followed by the distinctive cry of a seriously hurt child.

My heart pounded when I burst into the room. There was blood everywhere. Running down Jimmy's face, on the carpet, all over Keith's hands. And on the floor, spreading water and who knew what else onto my new carpet, was the nine-inch globe Nate had brought the boys from California the year before.

Both boys were screaming, tears pouring down their faces.

"Keith, in the bathroom, now!" Grabbing a shirt from the pile of clean laundry on his bed, I held it under my younger son's nose and with a hand on the back of his head, guided him to the bathroom across the hall.

"It hurts…" Jimmy wailed, his words barely discernible. *Please, God, don't let him have lost any teeth.*

"I know, baby," I told him, lifting him to the counter beside the sink. "Sit here and hold this while I look at your brother."

Sobbing, he took the shirt and did as I asked.

"No, Mommy, it hurts!" Keith screamed as I ran water in the sink and gently placed his hands beneath the faucet.

"I have to see how bad the damage is." I was having a hard time staying calm but I knew that, for them, I had to.

There were two cuts on Keith's hands that concerned me. Across each palm.

"What happened?" I asked when his sobs subsided.

"We bumped the wall and the shelf broke and I tried

to catch the globe but it broke and the wood hit Jimmy in the nose."

Jimmy let out another wail. His pupils weren't dilated, but I knew I should have him checked for a concussion. And a broken nose. Keith had to get stitches.

And my husband was off at a celebrity opening in Los Angeles, being wined and dined and entertained.

Where was Nate when I needed him? Jimmy's nose wasn't broken. The doctors weren't so sure about the concussion and were keeping him, at least for a few hours, for observation. Eyes wide with fright, he begged me not to leave him.

But I could hear Keith screaming in the next cubicle and had to hurry away. Thirty minutes later, I was sweating and exhausted from wrestling with a panicked child while a doctor put needles in his cuts. He had a total of fifteen stitches. Nine in one hand. Six in the other.

I called Nate's hotel from the emergency room. After I explained to a girl at the front desk that Nate's sons had been in a small accident and were at the hospital, she said she'd seen him leave about an hour earlier, but promised to see that he got the message as soon as he returned.

At the last minute I asked her to reassure him that both boys were going to be fine. Nate might not be here when I needed him, but he was exactly where I wanted him to be. Living out the chance of a lifetime.

I could handle stitches. Screaming boys. Nate had been there for me when we'd dealt with things I couldn't handle.

★ ★ ★

"Daddy!" I was signing insurance papers at the hospital's trauma unit desk almost eight hours later, preparing to take both tired boys home to bed, when I heard Keith's greeting.

"Daddy's here, Mom," Jimmy added, his voice a little weaker than his brother's.

I turned around and almost melted when my gaze locked on the tall, dark-haired, handsome but obviously harried man hurrying toward us.

He'd come. One phone call and he'd hopped on a plane to meet us at the hospital.

"Look, Daddy, I got fifteen stitches and can't take a bath for a whole week."

That wasn't entirely true. He couldn't get his hands wet. There were other ways to bathe him. But I decided this wasn't the time to impart the bad news.

"What's going on? What happened? Is everyone okay?"

Nate's questions came more quickly than I could answer them. He knelt down by Jimmy, scrutinizing the boy's swollen face.

"What's up, Jimbo?"

Jimmy looked like he might start crying again. "The globe hit me on the head. It *hurts.*"

"He's not concussed," I said before Nate could ask. "We've been here all day so they could watch him. The water globe you brought them last year fell off the shelf. Keith saw it falling and tried to catch it."

"Yeah, that's how I cut my hands." Keith, shorter and huskier than his younger brother, showed no sign of the fear he'd exhibited earlier.

Nate's eyes met mine again, and his were filled with apology. "I came the minute I heard," he said.

"I know."

Two weeks later, Nate sold his consulting business and with the money he made, plus a sizable bank loan, he bought a smaller, more family-oriented resort with minor ski slopes halfway between Denver and Boulder.

The day he drove me out to the resort and handed me the signed contract showed me, once again, how much my husband loved me. Loved all of us. He had no intention of missing any more of the important moments in our lives.

One of those moments, an unexpected one, came along the following year. I'd received my Colorado teaching certificate and filed it away. One afternoon in June of 1976, when I was home fingerpainting with the boys, now almost six and seven, a young woman knocked at my door.

She seemed familiar to me, but I couldn't figure out why. Tall and slender, in her early twenties, she smiled nervously. "Mrs. Grady?"

"Yes?" I had about three minutes before there'd be colors splattered on the kitchen tile.

"My name is Lori Gilbert."

Was the name supposed to mean something to me? The boys' voices floated in from the other room.

"Is your husband Nate Grady?"

"Yes." My voice, my whole being, grew hesitant. Dressed in jeans and a tie-dyed T-shirt, with long, dark hair and no makeup, my visitor looked more girl than woman.

But that certainly didn't mean she couldn't claim an association with my husband. She was only four or five years younger than I was. Yet I felt old, standing there barefoot wearing an old cotton smock over a sleeveless summer shift I'd had for several years.

"He's forty-one?"

"Yes."

"Mo-o-ommm!" Keith's battle cry.

"Coming!"

"Jimmy's throwing paint!"

"I am not!"

"James Grady, if I find one spot of paint on the floor when I get in there, there'll be no TV for a week."

The punishment was harsh. Unlike me. Born of a tension I created by this stranger on my doorstep.

"You have children?"

"Yes." I wouldn't give her any more than that. "Is there something I can do for you?"

The woman shifted an oversize denim bag on her shoulder. In some ways she looked more like a throwback to the sixties than a child of the seventies. Except that her clothes weren't loose and wild. And she wasn't wearing beads.

"I...um...you know..." She stopped. Smiled. And my heart began to beat faster. I recognized that mouth.

Had I seen her before?

Had she worked at the resort during my stint there after Sarah died? Or been a guest?

"This is a lot harder than I thought it would be," she said.

"Mo-o-ommmm! Keith's bossing me!"

"Listen to him!" I called over my shoulder, then turned back to the young woman. "Who are you?" I was out of time. Patience. Ever since Sarah's death things I would've taken in stride seemed to unhinge me.

"Have you ever heard of Holly Gilbert?"

"No." And I had a strong premonition that I didn't want to, either.

"She's my mother."

The boys were laughing. I told myself that I could always repaint the kitchen.

"She was married to Nate Grady."

I said nothing. Nate had never told me either of his previous wives' names. I'd overheard his conversation with Walt on my wedding day, when they'd referred to a Karen, but I'd refused to ask.

The woman licked her lips. "They were eighteen. It lasted a couple of months. Mom moved to New Jersey with her parents before she even knew she was pregnant. They agreed to help her, support us, if she promised not to get in touch with my father. My grandparents were afraid Mom and...Nate...would get back together and be miserable for the rest of their lives."

The drama in that last sentence revealed the girl's youth, so I concentrated on that for a few seconds.

But her story rang true.

"You're Nate's daughter."

"Yeah." She smiled again. And now I knew why I recognized her. She had Nate's mouth. And eyes.

"He doesn't know about you?" Somehow it was important to firmly establish that fact.

"Uh-uh." Lori shook her head.

"When did you learn about him? Being your father, I mean."

"Two weeks ago. I was helping Mom move and found some papers in a box in her bedroom. She always told me my dad died...."

I hated the woman. She'd robbed Nate of his first-born child. She'd *had* Nate's firstborn child.

"Would you like to come in?" I had no idea what else to say. To do.

"Are you sure it's okay?"

No. The world was rocking beneath my feet again. "Of course. Nate's at work. We own a small resort half an hour outside town. He runs a summer camp there."

She came into my home. I closed the door.

"How long have you been married?"

"Eight years." Didn't sound nearly as long or solid as it felt.

"How old are you?"

"Twenty-seven."

"Just four years older than me."

I didn't thank her for pointing that out.

Chapter 9

Nate was a little late getting home that night. This was his first year of offering a summer camp for kids at the resort, and with the place being so much smaller, a lot more rested on the venture.

He was tired when he pulled in. There seemed to be new lines on his face every day now. I watched as he parked our station wagon in the garage and stood at the edge of the lawn waiting for him.

To tell him that while our daughter was dead, he still had a daughter. Lori had asked me to be the one to break the news.

And I wanted to be the one. I wanted, at least, to have some part in this very major event in my husband's life.

I'd changed for the occasion, wearing my tightest pair of bell-bottom jeans and a halter top I'd bought but never had the courage to wear. I'd even put on some makeup.

I couldn't explain my actions, except that I was feeling threatened. And feeling as if I had very little ammunition with which to fight.

"What's up? Where are the boys?"

Briefcase in one hand, keys in the other, he stopped just inches from me.

"They're inside. Playing Candyland." *Don't worry, your daughter's in there watching them.*

In slacks and a polo shirt, with his broad shoulders, rock-hard stomach and thick, dark hair, Nate was every bit as handsome as he'd always been. The new lines on his face only added to that. To me, they were evidence of the experiences we'd shared.

I threw my arms around him, pressing my lips to his, wishing I could go back eight years, to my wedding night, and stay right there in that little piece of heaven.

He kissed me back, opening my mouth with his tongue and my response was eager—too eager for standing out on the driveway.

"Hey." He set down his briefcase, slipped his keys inside his pocket and pulled me fully against him. "What's this about?"

I was scared to death I was going to lose him. He loved his boys completely, but Sarah—a daughter—had held a unique place in his heart. And now he had a second chance.

"I have something to tell you."

"You're pregnant."

Hardly. We'd tried. But it just wasn't happening anymore. Maybe because Nate was older. Or because I'd been so upset by Sarah's death that I was somehow sabotaging my chances.

"No, but it's kind of like that."

His hands on my shoulders, holding me, the look in his eyes as he peered down at me like I was the only person alive, gave me the strength I needed to think only of him.

"I've got some good news for you, Nate." I smiled and my heart settled momentarily into that peaceful state I'd found so long ago. "At least I *think* it's good news...."

For him.

"You remember Holly Gilbert?"

His fingers tightened as he frowned. "Ye-e-ess. What's she got to do with this?"

"She gave you something twenty-three years ago and even though she didn't tell you about it, she took excellent care of it. Today, it arrived."

"A gift?" He sounded puzzled, as well he might.

I was botching this.

"You have a daughter, Nate. A beautiful, intelligent, kind and delightful young woman who has your eyes and your mouth. She's inside right now, sick with nerves while she waits to meet you."

"What!" His gaze darted to the house and back again. His frown deepened.

"Her name's Lori. Lori Gilbert. She spent the afternoon with the boys and me. You should see them with her. I'll bet that if she told them to eat spinach, they would."

"Holly and I didn't have a child. We were hardly married."

"She was pregnant when she moved to New Jersey with her parents. They agreed to help her on the condition that she not tell you about the baby."

"The hell they did!"

"There's no doubt she's yours, Nate. You only have to look at her to see that. Or…" I paused, swallowed the tears that wanted to interrupt my tentative composure. "Look at the baby picture she brought. She's so much like Sarah, it's…it's as if our precious baby's back again."

And in a way, for Nate, she was.

He watched me for a long time, as though trying to get right inside my heart. I tried, silently, to reassure him that I was fine—when I wasn't sure I was. I wanted him to know he had my complete support. No matter what.

And then he glanced at the house again.

"Go to her."

I waited outside. Lori deserved to have her father's undivided attention—or at least not to have Nate worrying about me, about how his actions might affect me as he met his daughter for the first time.

Crazy as it was, I felt inadequate, as though I'd somehow failed him where Holly had succeeded. I wondered if they'd be in touch now that they shared a child. And at the same time, I was genuinely happy for him. I loved Nate far more than I loved myself. He was a good man.

A great man.

I remembered how he'd sacrificed his own needs for mine after Sarah died—holding in his own grief and taking on mine, as well. And I knew he needed this.

Thirty seconds after he disappeared, Nate poked his head out the back door.

"Liza?"

"Yeah?"

"Come in here. I don't want to do this without you."

I climbed the steps slowly.

"I thought you were right behind me."

"I wanted to give you time alone with her…."

"Time alone is not time apart from you," he said softly, wrapping his arms around me as we stood for a moment on the back porch. "You're part of me, Liza. A vital part. Whatever happens to me, happens to you. We do it together. Right?"

My eyes filled with tears and I nodded. I should have known. Should never have doubted. Nate and I were one. Had been since the night we met. Would always be. No matter what.

Lori entered our lives, staying with us most of that first summer so she and Nate could get to know each other, so she could spend time with her half brothers

and, she said, so she and I could become family, too. Her
advent was a blessing in so many ways. The boys adored
her and she them. She became a good friend to me. And
Nate had a daughter again.

It had taken him a while to get over his anger with
Holly for robbing him of the first twenty-three years of
his daughter's life, but he'd come around. Especially after
I pointed out that he'd hate himself if he messed up the
next twenty-three with regret.

Every night that summer, he beguiled Lori with
stories about his own life and questions about hers. Her
mother had remarried when she was three, and her step-
father was good to her. They'd never had other children.
He was a doctor, recently retired at fifty, and her parents
were vacationing in Europe for the summer before
coming home to settle in their new house off the Cape.

Lori had just graduated from Yale and been accepted
at Georgetown's law school.

Her appearance that summer freed me up to spend my
days with Nate at the resort, getting the camp up and
running—bringing me closer than ever to my husband.
Other than my brief stint as a maid after Sarah's death, I'd
never shared Nate's working life. I enjoyed it immensely.

And after Lori returned east to enter Georgetown and
the boys were back in school—Jimmy going full days,
starting that year—I continued to work at the resort as
Nate's assistant, and to volunteer at the women's shelter
in Denver.

The next winter, in February of 1977, on the same

day that San Francisco suffered its worst earthquake in ten years, James Kenneth Crowley, my father, passed away in his sleep. He was only sixty-eight.

Nate, the boys and I went to California for his funeral. The visitation at the funeral home was the first time any of them ever saw my father. And the last. I cried bitterly, grieving for all that had been lost. He'd never seen his grandsons or met the man I loved with all my heart. Regret was like acid in my stomach. I'd grown up in the past few years and knew that one day I'd see my daddy again. And that he'd welcome me with open arms.

My God would welcome me in His home again. I had to believe that.

The time with my mother and sisters and their families was good for the boys. And for me, too.

We got to meet William's girlfriend. At thirty-five, a year older than he was, she was a scientist with a pharmaceutical company. She'd never been married. She was quiet. Unassuming. And lovely. I told my brother he'd better marry her quick before he lost the best thing that ever happened to him.

He did just that, in July of the following year. July 20th to be exact. In a double ceremony with two very handsome eight- and nine-year-old ring bearers, and a twenty-four-year-old maid of honor, Nate and I also walked up the aisle, celebrating our tenth anniversary with a renewal of our vows.

I was twenty-nine. Much more seasoned than I'd

been when I married this man. My hair was longer, my hips a little wider, my mind a bit wiser, but my heart was just as certain.

The church was filled to capacity with William and Shelly's friends. We'd invited a few of my old high-school friends, too, including Patricia. Even Walt, Betty and Mary Blackwell came. Most important, my whole family, and of course Shelly's, were there to cheer us all on.

Nate played piano for the reception, which meant I spent a lot of time without a partner, but I didn't mind. I used those hours to visit with loved ones I seldom saw. And sat on the piano bench whenever I needed my husband close.

Toward the end of the evening, as the lights were dimming and the children were getting tired, Nate hit a familiar chord and I stopped in midsentence the conversation I was having with Patricia. Glancing over, I met his eyes—and held them as he sang.

My gaze never wavered clear through to the last chorus of "My Cup Runneth Over" although my husband's image blurred as my eyes welled with happy tears.

We'd come through so much, years of living and loving, and as I lay in my husband's arms the next night—back at Walt's cabin in Colorado, while our sons stayed with my mother in California—I could honestly say I was happy.

And looking forward to the next forty years with anticipation and gratitude.

* * *

In the winter of 1978, shortly before Christmas, President Jimmy Carter doubled the size of the country's national park system. That brought about a resurgence of interest in outdoor sports, and business at our little resort picked up so much we had to expand. Nate hired a manager, but he was too hands-on to leave the running of the resort to someone else.

He did take time, though, to teach the boys to ski. I fought him the whole way. I thought eight and nine was far too young, and feared broken legs and worse.

Unfortunately, I was outnumbered and my men took to the slopes—to be joined by Lori when she came out over her winter break.

By January, the four of them had skis strapped to my boots, too, and to my own surprise, once I got over the initial shakiness, I loved the sport I'd avoided for the first twenty-nine and a half years of my life.

As long as I stayed on the baby slopes.

I made the boys ski there with me that year, although Keith, the stronger and huskier of the two, was probably capable of doing more. He knew better than to push me on that one, though, and we waved off Nate and Lori as they took the more challenging runs.

I'd signed my sons up for piano lessons the previous summer and both continued to attend and to practice. Keith was the more talented of the two, not so much in the music-reading department—Jimmy had him beat on that—but my oldest son had clearly inherited some of his father's musical gift. If he heard a song Jimmy was practicing, he could usually manage to pick it out and find chords that complemented it.

The problem was in stretching his hands to play the chords. One of the tendons had been damaged by his injury a few years before, and I feared that would prevent him from ever enjoying the piano as much as his father did.

Nate and I told him he could quit piano lessons, but he refused, saying that if Jimmy could do it, he could, too.

I was proud of his determination.

Still, I began to dread the afternoons when he'd sit down to practice. More often than not, the session would be interrupted by frustrated pounding on the keys. I was afraid he'd built in his mind some idea that his father would be disappointed in him if he didn't succeed at the instrument. I knew Keith would rather die than let Nate down.

One afternoon in March of 1979, I was in the kitchen scrambling to find something to make for dinner. I'd forgotten to take the chicken out of the freezer before I'd driven the boys to school and headed to the resort to check last-minute details for a wedding that was taking place there that weekend. I was now in charge of overseeing all events. There'd been a glitch with the florist, and I'd been tied up until it was time to pick up Keith and Jimmy from school.

I'd decided on omelets with cheese and bacon when the banging started in the living room where we now kept the piano. I cringed, trying to tune out the discordance. And didn't immediately notice that the sound had changed, down to one note at a time, with an added percussion beat that sounded strangely like something cracking—over and over again.

Dropping the seasoning I'd been planning to put in the egg mixture, I ran for the living room just as I heard Jimmy's call.

"Mo-o-ommmm! Keith's breaking the piano!"

"I am not!" Keith called back. I was close enough, at that point, to hear his hissed "shut up" to his brother.

"Mo-o-ommm!" Jimmy called again. I'd reached the archway to the living room.

"Keith Armstrong Grady! What have you *done?* Get up off that bench! Go to your room! And don't ever, *ever* come out again, do you hear me?"

I rarely raised my voice to my children. I'd never shrieked at them before. Two sets of brown eyes stared up at me. Both mouths hung open.

"Now!" I said, my heart breaking as I saw the little white chips all over the floor—and the tiny, misshapen grooves at the end of almost every key.

"Both of you," I added when neither boy moved.

"But I didn't do anything," Jimmy said.

"Now!"

The boys jumped up and ran from the room. I sat down on the bench, rubbing my fingers along the jagged edges of the chipped ivory.

Nate cherished this old piano. He'd had it since he was a child. It was all he had left of the family he'd grown up with.

It was ruined.

And I felt responsible.

I had no idea how I was going to break the news to him.

"Where are the boys?"

Nate had already put his briefcase in our small home office. He'd washed his hands. And was standing in the kitchen watching me put the finishing touches on dinner. He'd just noticed the table set only for two.

"In their rooms."

"They're not coming down for dinner?"

"I told them they couldn't come down again—ever."

Nate's silence behind me was my cue. All I could think about was those unsightly keys on his beloved piano.

And the crumbs of ivory he'd see if he looked in the wastebasket beneath the sink.

"Mom?" Keith's voice was tentative—behind me on the stairs.

"I told you to stay in your room."

"I know, but is Dad home?"

"Yes, son." Nate moved to the bottom of the steps. "But if your mother said you have to stay in your room, then I suggest you get your butt back up there immediately."

I heard Keith turn on the stairs. And then stop.

"Mom? Can I tell Dad, please? I was the one who did it and I should be the one who he gets mad at."

For a nine-year-old, my son was pretty smart. He'd already figured out that I'd set myself up to deflect his father's anger.

And if he was mature enough to figure that out…he was right. He *should* be the one to tell Nate what he'd done.

"Okay," I said. "Come on down."

Keith's step was slow. Heavy. And my heart went out to him. He was a little boy dealing with a kind of frustration—a kind of fear—that had broken grown men.

"What's going on?"

Nate, his voice patient, stood in front of Keith.

The boy looked his father straight in the eye. "I broke your piano."

"Broke it how?"

"With your screwdriver and hammer."

Nate didn't move, but I could see the muscles in the back of his neck tighten.

"Maybe you'd better show me."

Looking as though he'd been sentenced to death, Keith led Nate into the living room, around to the piano, and pointed.

"See?"

Nate stared for a solid minute. I loved him so much for taking the time to collect himself, to handle the worst of his anger, instead of exploding on the boy.

"Why?" That was all he said.

"I was mad."

"At the keys?"

"At my hands." Keith's voice wobbled, his chin against his chest.

"Then I guess we need to get you some physical

therapy—see if we can stretch and strengthen what tendon you have left, huh?"

Keith's head jerked up, his eyes wide. "Can they do that, Dad?"

"I don't know, but I suspect there's something they can do. We'll call the doctor tomorrow."

That night, when the boys went to bed, my husband sat down at his piano and without hesitation began to play—just as he always had. The notes sounded perfect.

Chapter 10

In November, fifty-two Americans were taken hostage in Iran. Our country was in shock. We couldn't believe such a thing could befall any of our own. We were protected, weren't we? Wasn't that what being American meant?

But the world was changing, and America was, too. Anytime I started to feel secure in my life, something happened to remind me that the only protection any of us had was loving and being loved.

ABC launched a nightly "Iran Hostage" program that, in the spring of 1980, was renamed *Nightline*. We watched it every evening. And in May, our little family traveled to Washington, D.C. to see Lori graduate from law school. We took the boys to see everything—the Washington Monument, the Lincoln Memorial, the White House. We visited the proposed site of a Vietnam Memorial.

And I met Holly.

I'd expected the occasion to be fraught with tension (everyone's) and jealousy (mine). The worst part was the anguish I put myself through before it took place. The woman was still lovely at forty-five, slim with blond hair that curled around her shoulders. A little taller than I was, maybe a bit heavier, she was elegant, confident and so in love with her husband, Todd, that there was no doubt in anyone's mind that she and Nate had made the right decision when they'd ended their young marriage.

Nate's face was stiff at first, but he managed not to express his anger at his ex-wife for keeping Lori from him all those years. He and I took a long walk the night before we met Holly to talk about the way he felt.

And we found a private corner in the grounds of the hotel and necked for a while. Even after almost twelve years of marriage, that still seemed to do the trick. For both of us.

Lori had accepted a job with a private firm and would be staying in D.C., at least for now. Nate had been hoping she'd find work with a firm out west, closer to us, but he was proud of her accomplishments—and the honor bestowed on her with such a prestigious offer.

I was proud—and disappointed—too. I'd found a true friend in Lori Gilbert and had been looking forward to having her around for more than a visit. I'd been hoping to share the next phase of her life.

Still, the trip was good. Nate and I enjoyed our boys on a whole different level. Instead of having to constantly watch over them, caring for their physical safety every second of the day, we were starting to debate with them, to challenge their thinking. In spite of the climate of the world in which we were living, we spent a lot of time laughing.

I was sorry when our vacation came to an end. Keith would be eleven that summer, going into sixth grade in the fall, and I knew my life would be changing again. He'd want to spend more time with his friends than with me. And my opinions were going to be challenged more than they were blindly accepted. Slowly but surely my boys were growing up—and away from me.

On January 20, 1981, the day of President Reagan's inauguration, $8 billion in Iranian assets were released by the United States and the U.S. hostages were freed after 444 days in captivity—giving us all a sense of renewed hope. And on November 13th, almost two years later, the Vietnam Memorial was finally dedicated. The Wall had 58,027 names on it, the names of all the U.S. servicemen and women who'd lost their lives in the Vietnam war.

Keith's was among them.

I was sitting in the doctor's office that afternoon, watching the dedication on TV with the rest of the women waiting their turn—keeping my mind focused on bigger matters than my missed period. I was only thirty-three. Too young for menopause. But I couldn't possibly be pregnant.

It'd been eleven years since I'd had a baby. Eleven years without birth control. My sons were in junior high. My husband was three years away from fifty.

Pregnancy and babies no longer fit our lifestyle.

I prayed to God I didn't have cancer.

"Congratulations, Eliza! You're pregnant!"

Well, of course, she was kidding. Dr. Eleanor Brown was just lightening my tension. But... She wasn't laughing. In fact, she seemed completely serious.

"How far along am I?"

"About two months."

I did the math—backward. Nate and I had run away to Las Vegas for a weekend after the boys started school. I'd been having a hard time dealing with Jimmy's departure from elementary school.

I did the math again. In the other direction. A June baby.

"You're sure?"

"One hundred percent."

I should be doing something besides sitting there, but I was too shocked to figure out what.

My heart pounded with excitement. And dread. What if... I couldn't live through a second...

"What...um..." My lips were dry and I ran my tongue across them. "What happened to...Sarah... What are the chances of..."

Dr. Brown hadn't been my doctor then. But she knew my history. Had all my records.

"Next to none," she said. "Anything can happen, of course, but it's extremely rare for one woman to suffer two separate cases of crib death. It's not genetic, nor does it have anything to do with how you care for your child. It's just one of those inexplicable flukes of nature that are nearly impossible to understand— or accept."

I wouldn't ever understand it. I wasn't sure I'd even get to the point of acceptance. But whether I liked it or not I was going to be a mother again.

"You're young. Everything looks good. I see no sign of anything but a perfectly normal pregnancy." Dr. Brown was concluding our meeting. I'd have to get up and go soon.

I'd have to leave this little room where my secret was safe. Go back to my life—and the men in it—who'd be wanting their dinner. Expecting me to behave just like I did every other night of their lives.

"I won't need to see you again for another month We'll schedule an ultrasound for the month after that."

I rose to my feet, but didn't move. "I thought you said there wasn't a problem."

"There's not."

"Then why the ultrasound? I didn't have them with my other pregnancies." If there was any chance she suspected something amiss, I had to know. Immediately.

Dr. Brown smiled. "Miracles of modern medicine," she said. "It's been, what, ten years since you had a baby?"

I nodded. "Eleven."

"Technology has come a long way since then, and with it, more affordable equipment. Ultrasounds are as common as physical exams nowadays. They tell us a lot more, too. Not only will we be able to see the baby's placement, which will allow us to prevent possible birth complications, but we can watch his growth rate, predict delivery dates and even, if you're lucky, find out his—or her—sex."

"In two months? I'll know all that?"

"Most of it." The doctor pulled open her office door. "You'll only know if it's a boy or a girl if the baby's lying right. And even then, we can't always tell."

"Bring your husband next month," the kindly, middle-aged woman said. "I'd like to meet him."

"I don't know…."

We stopped just inside the door. "What?" the doctor asked. "You don't think he'll want to be involved?"

Nate? Of course he would.

"I'd rather not tell him yet. Not until we're sure I'm not going to miscarry or anything."

Not until I could figure out how to break it to my forty-seven-year-old husband that instead of our lives getting easier now that the boys were more self-sufficient, we'd be starting midnight feedings and the terrible twos all over again.

★ ★ ★

On Christmas morning, when I should've been in the living room, watching my sons rip into their new TI-80s—the calculator that could do everything but print—I was upstairs in the bathroom, throwing up.

I'd passed the point where miscarriage was a worry. Had my three-month checkup. And was just weeks away from finding out if I was having another son or a daughter.

For Christmas Nate had given me airline tickets to Hawaii. A real honeymoon, he'd said, just the two of us. To make up for the trip I'd been unable to take thirteen years before.

He'd misinterpreted my tears for joy.

Just before the close of 1982, *Time* magazine named their Man of the Year—the computer. Technology was taking over our lives. And our doctors' offices. As the date for my ultrasound loomed closer, now only two weeks away, I knew I had to tell Nate we were going to have another baby. Too much longer and he'd start noticing, anyway. I'd already gained a couple of pounds. I just prayed he wouldn't be too upset. Or worried.

Or wish he didn't have such a young wife. A woman his age would not have been in this predicament.

Lori called to say she wouldn't be able to make it out for New Year's like she'd hoped.

Nate was really disappointed.

His buddy Arnold, who hadn't visited us since his

marriage years before, had also been planning to come and had to cancel.

I began the last day of 1982 the same way I'd started every morning of that week—bent over the toilet. Three pregnancies and I'd had no morning sickness. This one was making up for it.

I retched, waited, sitting on the floor in front of the toilet with my head against the wall, retched a second time and got up. Face washed and teeth brushed, I'd be okay for probably twenty-four hours. More if I was lucky.

Opening the bathroom door, heading for my closet and the first pair of jeans and sweater I could find, I figured I could just about make it downstairs before anyone missed me.

Deciding between bologna and turkey sandwiches to put in the boys' lunches for their all-day sledding trip with friends, I took one final look in the mirror to make sure there was no evidence of my recent activities, and plowed right into Nate.

He was standing outside the door, hands on his hips, and not a hint of a smile on his face.

"Hi!" I squeaked. Damn it.

A stern look was all I got in response. I crossed to my closet, and he followed.

"Did you run out of oatmeal? I'll be down in a second."

"Eliza."

Jeans held in front of me, as though for protection, I turned slowly to face him.

"When were you going to tell me?"

Not now. Not like this. I'd been thinking more along the lines of a quiet dinner for two—me in a negligee I could still wear with pizzazz and a little wine for him. Or a lot.

Or maybe on the ski slope. After a great run. He'd feel ready to take on the world then. A baby might not seem so overwhelming.

The thoughts raced through my brain.

"Tell you what?" I asked in a shaky voice.

What if he didn't want the baby?

"You've been throwing up for at least a week that I know of. You're pale. You've lost your appetite. You've been preoccupied, obviously worried about something. When are you going to tell me what's wrong with you?"

The breath I'd been holding came out in a rush. He hadn't figured it out, after all.

"Wrong?"

"Come on, Liza." He pulled me down to the bed with him, kept my hand firmly in his. "We do things together, right? Everything."

"Yes."

"So when were you planning to tell me you're sick? I've waited—and worried—for days, but this can't go on. I don't care what it is, we'll fight it. But I have to know what I'm fighting."

My dear, dear Nate. I stroked his cheeks, the lines at the sides of his mouth.

"I'm not sick, Nate. And I'm so sorry I made you worry. I had no idea you'd noticed anything."

"I notice everything about you."

Not *quite* everything.

"But if you're not sick, then what's—"

I hadn't suffered from morning sickness with the other three, but that didn't mean Nate was unaware of that particular side effect of pregnancy.

He stared at me, mouth open, and I knew he understood. What I couldn't tell from his deadpan expression was how he felt about the news.

"We're having a baby, Nate," I told him, just because it felt like the words had to be said. To lie there between us so we could deal with them.

"A baby."

There wasn't even a hint of elation in his voice. None of the excitement I'd been feeling on and off since I found out.

"In June."

That would mean three summer birthdays.

"You're not sick."

"No."

"Thank God." Nate's shoulders sagged and I saw moisture on his lashes as he scooped me into his arms. "I was so scared, Liza," he said with a shudder. "So scared."

"I had no idea," I whispered.

He held me for a long time. Kissing me. Looking me over. Giving thanks. Neither of us said a word about the baby.

★ ★ ★

"I'll need those plane tickets."

I turned from the dirty cereal bowls in the sink.

"What?" The boys had just left in a friend's station wagon; they were going to a sledding park in Denver with four other eleven- and twelve-year-old boys. We could talk freely about the baby.

Nate picked up his keys.

"For Hawaii. The trip's in April. Obviously you won't be able to go."

I stared at him. That was all he had to say about the news I'd given him less than an hour before?

"Can I have them, please? I need to see if I can get a refund."

"Of course." I ran upstairs, grabbed the envelope from my dresser, brought it downstairs and handed it to him.

Tapping one end of it against his opposite hand, Nate looked as though he was about to say something, then apparently changed his mind.

"I'll see you tonight." With a brief kiss that missed my lips, he was gone.

Twenty minutes passed—the dishes were done and I'd moved on to laundry, before I remembered that, in anticipation of Lori's visit, he'd taken off the week between Christmas and New Year's.

New Year's Eve came and went, a quiet night at home with our sons, playing games, singing along with

Nate at the piano and avoiding all reflection on what the next year would bring. I stared at the keys Keith had chipped all those years ago, worrying about this new child. We were all in bed and asleep well before midnight. And a week later Nate still hadn't said anything about the baby. He asked how I was feeling, asked if everything was okay—and that was it. Wanting to give him time to adjust, I didn't push, but I latched on to those oblique references, inferring his love, his concern for me and the baby, his involvement in this unexpected phase of our lives, in those two questions. He repeated them daily.

He played the piano every night that week. I was falling asleep early, so I wasn't even sure what time he finally came to bed.

On the fifth day of 1983 Lori called.

"Eliza? I wanted to tell you first, before Mom or Dad, because I know you'll be happy for me."

My stomach jumped. "What's up?"

"I'm married!"

But we'd just spoken to her a couple of weeks ago! "Married!"

"That's why I couldn't come and visit you. We used my time off to go to Las Vegas and elope. He's a lobbyist, Liza. I met him during law school. He's handsome and funny and I love him very, very much."

Grabbing the cloth from the little metal bar beneath the kitchen sink, I rubbed at a spot of missed jelly on the Formica countertop.

"Does he love you?"

Why hadn't she introduced us when we were in D.C. for her graduation? Or even mentioned that she had a boyfriend? And if they'd known each other for so long, why the sudden urgency? Why a secret wedding?

"Yes."

I remembered how my family had reacted to my own marriage. "So tell me about him," I said and decided the rest of the counter could stand a wiping, as well.

"His name's Wayne Bowing. He's thirty-four. He's got a degree in political science from Harvard and has been working here ever since he graduated. He bought a little house not far from the Hill."

"Has your mom met him?"

"No."

I moved the canisters at the back of the cupboard, wiped beneath them. And behind them.

"And you've known him how long?"

"Four years."

"What aren't you telling me?"

"He's divorced."

"So was your dad when I married him." She knew that.

"As of December 23rd."

"The December 23rd we had less than three weeks ago?"

"Yeah. And…he's got three kids."

"You've been having an affair with a married man with three kids," I said flatly.

"Yeah."

Cloth in hand, I dropped into the kitchen chair closest to me.

"How old are they?"

"Ages two through seven. Two girls and a boy."

He'd had a child with his wife since he'd started seeing Lori.

"Have you met them?"

"Not yet."

"How about his parents? Or anyone else in his family?"

"His folks are flying in this weekend. I'll meet them then. But they know about me," she finished in a rush. "He hasn't been happy in his marriage for years," she said. "He kept trying to make it work, tried to stay for the sake of the kids. But all they did was fight and he finally decided it'd be best for the kids if he left."

I didn't know what to say. Warnings were too late. Judgment would do no good. And there was no point in sharing my premonitions of her future with a man who made his living convincing people to do things. A man who'd been unfaithful to a woman who'd borne him three children, who'd walked out on that same woman and those kids, who'd kept Lori and their marriage a secret until it was a fait accompli....

"When do we get to meet him?"

"I have a three-day weekend coming up in February." She named it. Post-ultrasound. "Can we come then?"

"Of course." I considered telling her about the baby, but didn't want to without Nate's approval. I hadn't told my family or anyone else for the same reason. And—maybe—I was just a little scared to hear their reactions.

Nate would be in his sixties before this baby reached high school.

"Eliza? Will you tell my father about Wayne and me?"

"Don't you think you should do that?"

"He'll take it better from you."

I wasn't so sure about that. But their father–daughter relationship was still new enough, tender enough, to be damaged by a conversation gone awry.

"I'll tell him tonight, but only if you'll agree to be home so he can call you."

"I'll go straight home from work and stay there."

"When do you plan to tell your mother?"

"We're meeting her for lunch today. Wayne wanted to be there."

He rose a notch in my estimation. I just hoped, for Lori's sake, that when we finally met the man, he'd continue the uphill climb.

And I thought about love—the kind that drove you to throw all rational behavior to the winds and follow your heart.

"Will he be home tonight, too?"

"Yes. Eliza? Be happy for me?"

I half-heartedly began to wipe the spotlessly clean table.

Chapter 11

"She's been having an affair with this guy practically the whole time we've known her."

Nate and I were in bed later that night. He lay flat on his back staring up at the ceiling, while I was a good six inches away, doing the same thing. But at least we were talking. "Yeah," I said.

"It's going to be damn hard to like him."

I turned my head. "As hard it was for my dad to like you?"

He was quiet, so I was, too, thinking back over the evening. He'd sworn some. Paced a bit. And then he'd called his daughter, welcomed his son-in-law to the family and told them both he was looking forward to seeing them the following month.

I knew how hard that had been for him. And I loved him for it.

Nate rolled over, his face close to mine, and laid his hand against my stomach. It felt so good there. "I'm struggling, Liza."

My breath caught. "I know."

"I find out my daughter's married and I'm going to be a father all in the same week."

"Neither of which was planned or expected."

"I'm going to be fifty before this baby's even potty trained."

I reached for his thigh. "You're in better shape than a lot of thirty-year-olds."

"People are going to think I'm his grandpa."

"So? When have we ever cared what people think?"

"I realize how selfish it is, but I was really looking forward to having you to myself."

And that was the crux of it. I kissed him. And then again. "I'm older now, Nate. Better at organizing my time. I know more. And we'll have the boys to help. They're old enough to babysit."

His hand strayed to my breast.

"I won't be so nervous about leaving," I continued. I'd had a lot of time to work things out in my head. "And I think we should set up a date night that's sacred. Just you and me, once a week, no matter what."

His caresses were growing more focused, and my body responded with all the vigor it always had.

"What if something happens? I almost lost you the last time."

His fear fed mine. "We'd face that risk whether we were having another child or not," I told him. "We just have to have faith in God and each other to see us through whatever tragedies might come into our lives."

He kissed me, then murmured, "I love you, Eliza Grady."

I didn't think about anything but Nate for a long time after that.

On January 29th, 1983, the movie *ET,* which had stolen my heart the year before, won at the 40th Golden Globe awards. And Nate and I found out we were having a girl. Another daughter. I was ecstatic. And terrified.

He was a rock.

I was a little worried about telling the boys, sure that at the very least, they'd be embarrassed. It took Jimmy a day or two longer to think it through, but in the end, they were both happy that our family was growing.

"It's kinda cool, isn't it, Mom?" Keith said one day in early February when he and I were alone after school while Jimmy had his piano lesson. "You getting another chance to have a girl. Almost like God understood how much you needed her and wanted you to be happy."

What was cool was having such a wonderful son and I told him so.

* * *

Lori's visit was pleasant. Nate didn't dislike Wayne as much as he'd expected to, but neither of us liked him as well as I'd hoped we would, either. The man seemed superficial to me, but Lori honestly seemed happy and in the end, that was all that mattered.

She was thrilled about the baby. Elizabeth, we were calling her. She said she was hoping for a baby of her own, soon.

Nate and I hoped fate would put that off for a while.

Elizabeth Mary Grady, with big blue eyes and her daddy's black hair, entered the world on June 15th, 1983.

This time around, Nate was the one who had difficulty leaving the baby, and we spent the first six months of Elizabeth's life at home. No vacations for us that year. Mom came for the birth and stayed for a couple of weeks. Alice, June, Bonnie and William, with their spouses, all visited at separate times that summer, too. Keith celebrated his fourteenth birthday on a white water rafting trip with a friend from school.

We didn't see Lori, or hear from her quite as often, but so far, she seemed happy. Based on what she shared with us, anyway. Thankfully there was no sign of a baby yet.

Jimmy became a teenager with a swimming and slumber party at the resort, chaperoned by his parents and two-month-old sister, and had the time of his life.

"Thanks, Mom," Jimmy said the next morning.

We were gathering the last of his presents from the suite, his long arms and legs gangly as he stood nose-to-nose with me.

I barely managed to keep from embarrassing him by starting to cry. I hid my emotion in a hug—which, surprisingly, he allowed with no squirming.

Nate turned forty-eight that year and at his annual physical exam, his doctor told him he had the heart and lungs of a much younger man. He played the piano for hours that night, serenading Elizabeth, who was perched close by in her baby seat, with lullabies, coaxing the boys into a rousing singalong of old hits most of their friends wouldn't even recognize, and covering all of my favorites, as well.

The news added bounce to his step—and renewed passion to our bed. I was nursing, and tired a lot, but eager, too.

The resort was doing well. My children were robust and healthy. And my husband made love to me at least four times a week.

I knew that if I'd been able to see everything that would happen in the years after leaving St. Catherine's, I would still have done it. Being Nate's wife, the mother of his children, was the perfect life choice for me. I'd found my purpose. My soulmate.

My life was blessed.

The following summer, a week before Elizabeth's first birthday, we had a call from Lori. She'd been offered a position at the London branch of a private firm whose home office was in D.C. and would be leaving almost immediately. Her husband would not be going with her. She'd filed for divorce.

I didn't ask, but I suspected she'd caught him with another woman.

May 31, 1985 was a day I would never forget. Forty-one tornados hit the northeastern United States, killing eighty-eight people. I was glued to the television set in the kitchen while my almost two-year-old precocious daughter climbed up the kitchen drawers she'd pulled out. By the time I noticed, she was standing on the stove, reaching for the cupboard where I kept a small candy stash for the boys.

"Elizabeth! No!" I shrieked behind her, scaring her probably as much as she'd just scared me. She lost her balance and would've fallen if I hadn't somehow made it across the room to catch her.

"Canee, Mama." Her eyes were wide, her brow furrowed as she stretched one arm for the cupboard.

"Absolutely not." My recovery was not nearly so quick. "You are never to climb up there again, do you understand me?"

"Canee?" Her babyish lilt took on the higher note that indicated imminent tears.

"No. You were naughty, and naughty girls don't get candy." And thank God your father didn't walk in to

see that, I added silently. Nate worried too much as
it was.

If he had his way, Elizabeth would live her life in a
playpen.

The idea didn't sound so bad at the moment.

After a tight squeeze and a kiss, I put the baby down.

"Canee?" She lifted her tiny hand skyward.

"No, Mommy can't give you candy right now."

Elizabeth's chin puckered and her lips turned down.
I wanted to scoop her up and give her the entire bag of
licorice she knew was in the cupboard. Instead, I
watched as she plopped down hard on her diapered
behind and started to cry.

I brought her with me into the laundry room after
that, keeping her safe in a pile of towels at my feet as I
sorted clothes. And had to stop twice to rescue her—
once when she found the cord to the vacuum cleaner
behind the door and tried to take it apart, and the second
when she tried to unscrew the foot from the bottom of
the dryer and got her hand caught instead. If this child
made it to her third birthday without a trip to the emergency room, it would be a miracle.

Grabbing the last pair of Nate's pants, shoving my
hand into the pockets out of sheer habit before throwing
them in the washer, I happened upon a piece of paper.
Usually, if I found anything, it was coins.

Thinking I'd hit the jackpot with a dollar bill, I
pulled it out.

"What did Daddy leave us?" I asked the curly-headed little girl playing with my big toe, which peeked through the top of my sandal.

I ended up with a receipt, went to toss it, then figured I'd better make sure it wasn't something he needed. A business expense. Or the bill for some item he might want to return.

He'd purchased two glasses of wine. One white and one red. From a restaurant I didn't recognize.

Nate didn't drink wine. Except, on very rare occasions, with me. His choice of alcoholic beverage was either beer or whiskey and soda.

He'd used his personal credit card.

And it was dated two days ago—at 7:16 p.m.—when Nate had arrived home from Denver more than an hour late because of a traffic jam on the highway.

With a knot in my stomach, I stared at the baby gurgling happily on the floor, her earlier disappointment long forgotten as she pulled at the lace on her tennis shoe. She was busy, full of constant energy, completely secure. She trusted that she'd be loved and tended to twenty-four hours a day.

She adored her daddy.

And he adored her.

I wadded up the receipt and threw it away.

I went upstairs early that night—telling the boys not to stay up too late. Elizabeth was asleep in her crib and shouldn't need me again until morning. Pouring rose-scented bubble bath in my tub, I ran the water, stripped and got in. I soaked until my skin was silky. I shaved. And when I got out, I sprayed Nate's favorite perfume on my throat—and my breasts.

And then, feeling desperate and a bit naughty, I slid, completely naked, beneath the covers to wait for my husband to come to bed.

More than an hour later, I was still lying there, wide awake, when I heard him come upstairs, pause by each of our children's bedrooms—checking on them as he always did—before continuing to our room.

"I thought you'd be asleep," he said as he entered.

Or *hoped I had?* I wondered, but pushed the thought away. It was unfair.

I shook my head. My hair, cut shorter since Elizabeth's birth, was no longer damp from my bath. "I was waiting for you."

He looked surprised but not unhappy with my response. "What's up?" he asked, throwing his clothes in the laundry bin as he undressed.

"Nothing."

He glanced over at me, then disappeared into the bathroom. I heard the water running as he brushed his teeth. I'd planned to be sitting up with the covers about my waist when he came in but I'd chickened out.

Now I wished I'd put on my nightgown. What if he climbed into bed and turned over without even finding out that I was lying there naked?

Or worse, found out and wasn't in the mood to make love.

But if I got up now and he caught me walking naked to my dresser, I'd feel even more stupid.

This whole come-on thing was new to me and I was quickly becoming aware that I wasn't good at it.

Squirming under the covers, I cursed my lack of experience. The room was lit by one small light on Nate's side of the bed. And the soft illumination cast a golden glow on his skin as he came in from the bathroom. He'd shed his underwear.

And was already big.

My body surged with desire and all self-consciousness fled as I openly perused Nate's nakedness. I stuck a leg out from underneath the covers, giving him a glimpse of my thigh. Over the past months I'd slimmed back down to my prebaby weight and was confident that my husband would find no fault with my body.

One glance at that thigh and Nate, reaching the bed, yanked at the covers, pulling them down to the bottom of the bed. I was ready enough for him that I welcomed the exposure.

"Make love to me, Nate," I said, my voice husky with need. If fear was there, too, he needn't know.

Unlike the rest of me, my breasts hadn't gone down to prebaby size when I'd weaned Elizabeth, as they had with the other children. I lifted my shoulders, proud of them.

He didn't hesitate as he lay down with me, immediately taking one of my nipples into his mouth.

I touched Nate in ways I'd never touched him before that night. Climbing on top of him, kissing him, following my instincts as some integral part of me sought to claim him as solely mine.

To show him I could please him to the point of exhaustion. That he didn't need anyone else.

I don't even know where my hands and mouth and body had learned the things I did that night, but when we lay together, sweaty and wet and spent a couple of hours later, I was happy again.

"I love you," I said, my face against his chest as I drifted off to sleep, cuddled securely in his arms.

He'd fallen asleep. But he was at home, in bed with me, naked, holding me.

For that night, it was enough.

Two weeks later, just before our daughter's second birthday, I came into the master bedroom after putting Elizabeth down for her nap to find Nate in the bathroom, bent over the sink. The boys were at the resort, helping out with summer camp for the younger guests. Nate had come home after a morning in Denver to have lunch with me before going in to work.

He'd been doing that a lot more lately—stopping by the house to spend unexpected moments alone with me. The fear that had taken hold of my heart when I'd discovered that receipt was slowly receding.

"What're you doing?" I asked, my hands on his shoulders as I peered around him.

He had a pair of his underwear beneath the water and was scrubbing at a spot with a bar of soap.

"Is that blood?" I asked, dropping my hands to come around beside him. Was something wrong?

Fear of a new kind took root inside me. I glanced down at his clothed lower body, my mind running through possibilities. Things like a urinary tract infection. Or a bug bite.

But the smear was too large for that. And shaped like...

I glanced up then, and when I met the stricken look in Nate's eyes I knew. The stain was in the shape of a woman's lips. It was lipstick.

Not mine.

As stupid as it sounds, I was completely stunned. I'd managed to convince myself that there'd been some logical explanation for the receipt I'd found—done such a thorough job of hiding from the truth that I hadn't even bothered to share my discovery with Nate.

Without a word, I turned and left the room, but didn't know where to go. Shaking, panicked and dizzy, I stood in the middle of our room, my arms wrapped around myself, and couldn't move.

"Liza..."

Nate came in, reached toward me, but let his hand fall.

"Who is she?" I managed to ask.

"No one. She's no one important."

And that's when my heart broke. He didn't deny her existence.

I had nothing else to say. Life as I'd known it had just ended.

"Talk to me, Liza."

I'd left the bedroom, couldn't stand to be there with him, with the bed we'd shared for sixteen years, and the memory of what I'd done with him such a short time before. I was in the living room, standing almost exactly as I'd been in the bedroom.

Nate sat down on the edge of the couch, his hands clasped in front of him. I wondered, perhaps inanely, what he'd play if he sat down at the piano now.

What songs did he play when he thought about her?

"I'm sorry, Liza. So sorry. I don't know what happened, how it got so far out of hand. I love *you*."

"I don't believe you." He would never have done this to me if he'd had me anywhere close to his heart.

"She's chairman of the Funds for Kids auction."

A charity function held annually in Denver to raise money for needy kids. We'd been donating a week at the resort for the past few years.

This year we were hosting the auction. A function that would've been my responsibility except that I hadn't returned to work after Elizabeth was born.

I'd never met the woman my husband had been working with so closely.

"How long has it been going on?" It didn't matter. I just seemed compelled to jam the knife in further.

"Not long."

"How long?"

"I met her in January."

I turned at that. "You've been sleeping with another woman since *January*?"

"No!" Nate's eyes were moist. I tried not to care. "We met to talk about the auction."

"How many times have you slept with her Nate?"

"I don't know!"

That many.

"I didn't count because it didn't matter," he said. "A few times. Not many."

"Is she married?"

"Divorced."

"Young?" I just kept twisting the knife. I wasn't a kid anymore. And Nate liked them young, I thought bitterly. Look at how he'd gone after me when he'd practically been old enough to be my father.

"No! She's my age."

I couldn't believe it. It didn't fit. Young wasn't good enough? The age barrier between us suddenly grew to insurmountable heights. This was something I couldn't fix.

Chapter 12

"I'm sorry it happened, Liza." Nate still sat on the couch, clearly troubled. Penitent. Not begging, not defensive, just honestly sorry.

I discovered that sorry wasn't enough.

"Do you love her?"

"No. I'm completely in love with you."

I didn't want to hear that—didn't want him confusing me. I had to get through this and find the other side. Elizabeth would be waking up soon. Needing a mother. The boys would be home for dinner. I had roles to play. Responsibilities. "Then why?"

He shook his head. "I've been asking myself the same thing. And I have no excuse other than that I've been feeling so old lately. I'm turning fifty this year. That's half a century."

"So? Age never mattered to you before."

"You run after Elizabeth and still have energy for the boys and games and cleaning, and making love all night. I take care of her for an afternoon and I'm ready to fall asleep in front of the TV. I yearn for quiet, expensive dinners in adult company. You thrive when Elizabeth's throwing food."

Not really, but there didn't seem to be any point saying so.

"Let's face it. I'm growing old and you aren't and it's bothering me."

We were all growing older. Every second, with every breath.

"My age threatens you?"

"No. Mine does when I'm with you."

"But not when you're with her."

"I've never been *with* her," he said, though I had no idea why. He'd been *with* her in every sense of the word. Her lipstick was on his underwear.

The thought twisted me up all over again.

"We've met for the auction and two or three times we've done more than talk about the auction. That's it. We've never gone anywhere together, made plans or talked about anything that really mattered. But no, to answer your question, I don't feel so over the hill when I'm with her. I don't feel like I'm going to die long before she does."

"I could die in a car wreck tomorrow."

"And if you live a normal life span, you'll be spending the last ten or fifteen years of your life without me." His voice was firm. His gaze straightforward and intense. "When you're most frail, most needy, I won't be there. Do you know what that does to me?"

"It's a choice I made when I married you, Nate. You think I didn't know that? Wasn't prepared for it?"

"I didn't think about any of this very much until Elizabeth came along."

In one small part of my heart, I could understand. But I was too shattered to hold on to that.

Still… "Have you told her it's over?"

His silence was my answer.

"When's the last time you were with her?"

"Liza, don't do this. I'll call her right now, tell her to hold the auction someplace else."

I didn't care about the damned auction.

"Today, Nate? While I was home this morning making beds and changing diapers, were you in Denver screwing another woman?"

I couldn't believe how I was talking. Didn't recognize the ugly, bitter tone in my voice.

Nate didn't answer.

"Why didn't you just throw the damned underwear away?" I railed.

"I don't know."

I rubbed my arms, became aware of the cramping in my calves. I'd been standing in the same position too long.

"Do you have plans to see her again?"

"I'll cancel them."

He'd been expecting to see her again. If I hadn't come into the bathroom, caught him, he would've continued to have sex with us both. Not only had he not ended it, he'd had no plans to do so.

And that severed what was left of any feeling inside me. Killed it off as if it had never been.

"Pack a suitcase and get out, Nate." I could find no anger. No hurt. Just cold, calm thought. "Out of this house. Out of my life." It was one month before our seventeenth anniversary.

He jumped up, came toward me—the strong, caring man I'd known and loved all these years. The man I'd laughed with, made love with, grieved with and almost died with.

A man I didn't even recognize. And would never trust again.

"Liza…"

"*Now,* Nate."

I didn't move.

He did.

And within twenty minutes, while our infant daughter still napped in her crib, he was gone.

I slept on the couch that night, unable to lie in the bed I'd shared with Nate—to lie there alone—to lie there knowing that while I'd touched him so intimately, allowed him to touch me in ways no one else had, he'd also been touching someone else.

And letting her touch him.

I couldn't get past that part. I'd thought the one thing sacred between Nate and me—the one thing we shared with no other person—was our intimate, sexual selves. Our hearts, our minds, our time, our arms and hands and feet we took into the world with us. But not that which made us male and female.

I turned on the television for the first time that day. TWA Flight 847 had been hijacked with 153 passengers and crew aboard. Nineteen passengers had been released as a trade for fuel, and another twenty at the next stop. The rest, 114 men, women and children, including a U.S. Navy diver, remained in captivity.

Thinking about those people still trapped in their airliner seats, about a world where unspeakable things happened, about lives that went on for years and years and then, without warning, were irrevocably broken, I couldn't feel anything but the same detached horror I'd known all day.

When the news started repeating itself, I turned off the set.

What continued to haunt me was that not only had Nate been unfaithful to our marriage vows, he'd done so while still enjoying the benefits of that marriage. He'd made me part of a triangle without giving me a choice. If he'd had her at a time when he and I had not been intimate, I might've been able to get beyond what he'd done. But he hadn't. He'd gone back and forth between the two of us. Back and forth. Touching me. Touching her.

Sliding down on the couch, I stifled a cry. Nate might be free tonight, might even be with her, but I had children upstairs. Sons who were confused and shocked and hurting, too.

And a little girl who still trusted him.

Nate wasn't perfect. He was human. He'd stood by me through a lot of hard times. Given beyond what was fair.

Had I acted too hastily?

Was this how Jane Eyre had felt after she'd left Mr. Rochester? I'd always rushed through that part of the book.

Maybe I just needed to open up, to be a little freer in my thinking. Join the 1980s. Understand that Nate was struggling. Afraid.

But it was more than that.

My mind wandered back and I was nineteen again, sitting in a bar down the street from St. Catherine's, wondering whether my decision to join the convent had been the right one. Realizing it was.

And later, when I sat in my room at the convent days before moving to the mother house, when I answered Nate's letter and read what I wrote—*Yes, I'll marry you*—my heart had again known peace.

Tonight, lying alone on the couch Nate and I had chosen together several years before, I also knew I'd made the only choice that was right for me that day—telling Nate to leave.

Beyond the body, beyond everything, even love, was *trust*.

Nate's struggle, his fear, his temptation, I could understand. But he'd crossed a line that prevented us from ever going back to where we'd been. Instead of coming to me, telling me he was having problems, letting me be a part of the solution, or at least share in his pain, he'd gone to another woman.

Nate had broken my trust. He'd done it knowingly. And he'd done it repeatedly.

Without trust, there was nothing.

I didn't tell anyone, other than my boys, for some time. It was summer. I was no longer working outside the home. Hiding was easy. Easier than facing the future. It had no definition. No promise of magic. That first month, I focused on getting up in the morning. Changing and dressing Elizabeth, making breakfast, listening for Nate's car in the drive as he came to take the boys to work at the resort. Breathing again when he was gone. I did the dishes and laundry and housework, fed Elizabeth, did more dishes, put her down for a nap. And every single day, that was when I faltered.

I had two hours to fill. Two hours that haunted me. Two hours to replay those hours that had changed my life.

Then Elizabeth would get up again. I'd play with her. Fix dinner. Wait to hear Nate's car a second time. He never came in. And I never looked out.

I avoided the piano like the plague—turning my head

away from it anytime I was in the room. I couldn't bear to look at those broken keys.

At the end of the first week, Keith entered the kitchen carrying an envelope with my name on it, made out in Nate's handwriting.

"Put it on the counter," I said to my son. "Dinner's ready."

We were having lasagna. With homemade pasta. Making it had consumed most of Elizabeth's two-hour nap that day.

"Dad said I should give it directly to you." Keith stood in middle of the kitchen, envelope in hand, his gaze resolute.

Too much like his father's.

"In this house, what I say is what happens. And I said to put it on the counter."

A spark of hurt appeared in my oldest son's eyes before he lowered his lids and did as I asked.

"I'm sorry, Keith." I turned from the sink and held out a hand. "Give it to me."

Keith could have told me to get it myself. It was what I deserved. He collected the envelope and handed it to me instead. And stood watching, his eyes seeing far too much.

Hoping he didn't notice my shaking hands, I slit open the envelope, my mind slipping back to the day Nate's first letter had come for me at the convent. I felt about as sick now as I had then.

Was he asking to come back? Would I let him?

Or was this a request for the clothes hanging on his side of the closet? The ones in his drawers upstairs?

Was he coming to collect his things?

The single piece of paper was too small to fill the envelope. And there was no letter from my husband. It was a check. And the memo line merely said *Eliza's share of week's pay-out to owner.* It was more than three quarters of our usual income. Either he was siphoning money from the company—which I knew instinctively he was not—or Nate was living on very little money.

The idea brought tears to my eyes. Nate had always been so generous....

But then a voice that had appeared insidiously in my head this past week reminded me he didn't need a lot of money if he was living in someone else's home, sleeping in her bed, eating at her table.

The boys hadn't said where he was. And I didn't ask.

"Tell your father thank you," I said to Keith. Jimmy came in then, stopping to play patty-cake with Elizabeth, who was in her high chair, and I put the plates on the table.

On the last day of June, 1985, the remaining hostages from TWA Flight 847 boarded a U.S. military plane and were flown to West Germany. Nate had been gone two weeks and one day. I lay there in our bed alone, watching the hostages reach freedom, and out of the blue, with no warning, I began to feel again. An onslaught spread through me. I thought at first it was joy as I lived those glorious moments of release with the men and women who'd been caught in a hell I could only imagine. But suddenly, cruelly, joy was replaced by all the feelings that had been trapped inside me, waiting to be set free. The pain was so severe I couldn't breathe.

And then I started to cry. Huge, racking sobs that shook my body, my bed. Shook me to the very core. I gasped for breath, only to have it taken from me by the next wave of anguish. I had to stop. Tried to stop. But every moment of calm became an opportunity to fill me up with more despair.

I had thought I'd suffered the worst life had to offer after Sarah died. I'd been wrong. As unbearable as that time had been, through it all I'd been wrapped in love. A security that allowed me the space to grieve.

This was why I hadn't cried. Now…I was never going to stop.

"Mom?"

I held my breath at the sound of Keith's tentative voice. Perhaps he hadn't heard me. Perhaps he'd think I was asleep.

"Mom?" The second voice was closer. And louder, too. Jimmy didn't have the finesse of his older brother.

"Go away."

The mattress dipped on either side of me.

"It's going to be okay, Mom." Keith's voice had changed over the past couple of years. At first, it used to squeak sometimes, but it had become deep, grown-up, without my really noticing.

"Keith and I can do anything Dad would do around here," Jimmy said. At nearly fifteen, he was still at the squeaking stage.

I didn't have the heart to argue with him. I rolled onto my back instead, reaching out a hand to each of my sons.

"You boys have a lot to do. You don't need to be playing nursemaid to me," I told them, finding a smile. "I appreciate the offer, and I'm sure I'll take you up on it now and then, but I don't want you thinking you have to assume the responsibilities of grown men. Your time for that will come soon enough."

I'd lost the life I'd built for myself; I was not going to have them lose theirs, too.

"We're lucky to have income from the resort and while it's not making us millionaires, there's enough to support us all." Two households, I was thinking but didn't say aloud. I thought Keith understood. "And to send the three of you to college."

"These things happen all the time," I added, and named a couple Nate and I had socialized with a few years back. Jimmy named a woman who'd just started as a reservations clerk at the resort. Keith named the parents of one of his friends. All people whose circumstances we knew.

I glanced at my sons' solemn faces in the half-lit room.

"All three of those families have to adjust to far bigger changes than we do—the mother being at work all day.

Or a reduced income. Or the kids not seeing their dad anymore." I paused. "We don't. We're really very lucky."

I'd repeated the word *lucky*. A word I didn't feel at all. And yet, as I spoke to my sons, I encouraged myself, as well. My heart was broken, but it could be worse. Much worse. My entire home could be broken, too, and it wasn't.

I needed to concentrate on that.

And be thankful.

I often thought about underwear these days. Nate's underwear. Who was seeing it. Washing it.

Kissing it.

I'd be minding my own business, cooking some new concoction the boys were going to stick up their noses at but eventually eat, doing their laundry, teaching Elizabeth to count, cleaning up after the active two-year-old, or watching movies with my sons, and suddenly I'd have a vision of Nate standing in our bathroom with stained underwear in his hands.

I'd see again the stricken look in his eyes.

And I'd sink into the well of darkness that was my constant companion.

Still, I had to live. I had children to take care of.

It occurred to me one evening, as I kneaded bread to go with the peach jam I'd made that afternoon, why Nate hadn't thrown that underwear away. A part of him had *wanted* to get caught. He'd wanted me to find them.

As his way of telling me what he couldn't bring himself to say?

Hurting me would've been nearly impossible for Nate to do. I'd always believed that.

But then, if it was so impossible, he wouldn't have been able to take his clothes off for another woman. He must've at least thought of me as held her, positioned himself above her. Entered her.

He must have noticed where she was different from me. Felt different. Responded differently.

"Hey, Mom. Let me do that."

I jumped guiltily as Keith came up beside me, more thankful than ever that my son couldn't read my thoughts.

And disappointed in myself for having them—once again.

Chapter 13

"**Y**ou want to make bread?" I covered my embarrassment with the question. Last I'd known, Keith had been playing an arcade game on the television with Jimmy. My mother had sent them an Atari box with two controls and a series of games the previous Christmas.

"What do I do? Just beat the thing?"

I'd been pounding down the dough when he walked in.

"No," I said, wondering what had motivated this generosity. "Dust your hands with flour and I'll show you," I said, and watched as my broad-shouldered son, huskier than his father and younger brother, put his muscles behind a wad of dough.

"I was thinking," he said as he worked up enough flour dust to coat his face and clothes, and half the floor, as well. "I'm going to be sixteen next week."

I nodded. We'd talked about going out to dinner to celebrate.

"And with Dad gone and all, I thought it'd be good for me to get my driver's license before school starts. That way I can take Jimmy to school so you don't have to cart Elizabeth out—especially when it gets colder."

Jimmy could also take the bus. Not that either of them had ever had to do that.

"You're signed up for driver's ed for the fall semester."

"I know. But Richard was telling me about this class you can take that goes all day every day for two weeks and then you're done. There's a session scheduled for the first of August."

No! my mind screamed. So loudly I could hardly hear any other thoughts. I couldn't put my baby out on the road with all the maniacs. Not now. Not so soon.

Not while I waited here all alone.

"You have to work," I said through stiff lips.

"I would've missed work if we took a summer vacation like we talked about."

Before Nate left. We'd considered a trip to California to see my mother.

"How much does the class cost?"

He told me, and the price was actually lower than I'd expected. Damn it. "I've got enough saved from working this summer to pay for it," he said.

He was Nate's son there.

Keith continued to knead, and although the bread was going to be denser than I'd wanted it, I didn't stop him.

"The class, the license, is all fine and good, Keith, but that's only the beginning. There's not much point if you don't have a car. Which you don't. And then what about insurance? And gas?"

"If you say yes to the class, I was planning to ask Dad for a car. He always said he'd help me get my first car. And right now, I kind of figure he owes us, you know?"

The boys never mentioned their father—either positively or otherwise. And neither did I.

I wasn't going to be one of those women who badmouthed their father to her children. Keith and Jimmy needed Nate. Elizabeth did, too. Being a rotten husband didn't make him a bad father.

"There's still the gas and insurance."

"With the money I've saved I can just about swing the insurance. And, Mom, I was thinking I could either work weekends at the resort for gas, or ask you for it since I'll be doing the driving you'd have been doing anyway."

He'd thought it all through. So well my head was spinning. And before I could stop and think of a way out, I'd agreed.

My firstborn was going to have his license. His freedom. He wasn't going to be as dependent on me ever again.

I couldn't sleep that night. I tried to read, but neither

of my faithful companions—*Jane Eyre* or my Bible—was able to comfort my unsettled heart.

My mom called to wish Keith a happy birthday. I still hadn't told her about Nate. And decided this wasn't a good time to do it.

I'd also neglected to tell my siblings.

Lori called, too, the next day. For the same reason, I assumed. Keith was at work, but he'd be glad to hear she'd phoned.

Genuinely pleased to hear from her, missing her, I greeted her the way I always did. Asked how she was doing.

"My dad just called."

I slid down to the kitchen floor. "Oh." I'd been about to hit the cookbooks again, to occupy naptime with a new, more challenging recipe for dinner. I'd bought a book on gourmet cooking at the mall in Denver over the weekend and read it late Sunday night.

"I can't believe you didn't tell me!"

The boys wouldn't love spinach soufflés.

"You've got your own stuff to deal with." And I still couldn't talk about what had happened between Nate and me.

"All the more reason you should've called! I can't *believe* my dad," she said, sounding a lot angrier than I felt. "He's just like Wayne. A jerk. An absolute jerk."

I didn't know what to do.

"What did he tell you?" I asked.

"That he slept with some woman in Denver he'd been working with on a charity deal."

"Yeah." If *slept with* meant more than once.

"I'm so sorry, Eliza. You don't deserve this at all."

"Life isn't about fairness and deserving, honey." I told her the one thing I'd managed to figure out, in case it could help her. "It's about living. And learning."

If I concentrated on Lori, on the fact that she'd revealed what I'd suspected all along, that Wayne had been unfaithful to her, I could get through this.

"What about *loving?*"

I didn't have an answer to that.

"He resigned from hosting the auction," Lori said.

That must have endeared him to his lady friend.

"He's got a suite at the resort."

My heart sank. So everyone there knew. That somehow made it official, his leftover clothes in my closet notwithstanding.

"He asked me to call you."

"He shouldn't put you in the middle like that. You tell *him* to call me if he needs something." Maybe I should wake Elizabeth from her nap, go to the park or a pool someplace.

The only pool I knew of was at the resort.

"He wanted me to call for you, not him. Said you probably hadn't told anyone about this, that you were handling it all by yourself. I want you to know that my loyalty lies with you, Eliza. Yes, he's my father, but you've both been family to me and he's dead wrong here. I've told him the same thing."

I started to wonder how he took that. But stopped myself. I didn't need to wonder. I knew. Nate would have seen the fairness in Lori's response. He would've been proud of her.

"He's your dad, Lori, and you've been without him for most of your life. Don't lose him again."

"I won't. But you have all my support, Eliza."

Tears sprang to my eyes and I wiped them away. "Thank you."

"You're welcome. Now, I had this idea…"

I don't quite know how it happened, but somehow, before I'd hung up the phone, I'd agreed to a seven-day trip to London, to visit my almost ex-stepdaughter for a week before school. Nate had said he'd stay with the kids.

And while I was gone, he moved his stuff out of our house.

Except for the piano.

School started again. This year I had two sons in high school as Jimmy entered his freshman year. I didn't file for divorce. There was no reason to. I was a one-man woman and I'd had him. Whatever else life held in store for me, it wasn't going to be another relationship. Another marriage. I didn't have the interest.

I didn't have the heart.

I knew Nate would file. He'd had his fiftieth birthday that fall and would want to get on with his life. Sometimes I dreaded seeing the mail, dreaded seeing the letter from his attorney. Yet sometimes I approached the mailbox with a strange kind of hope.

I wanted it over and done with.

I was tired of hurting.

Of waiting.

My mom called to say she was coming out for Thanksgiving, and I was finally forced to tell her that Nate and I had separated. She didn't say much, just suggested the kids and I fly out there for Thanksgiving instead.

We did. And the support my family showered on me—on us—went a long way toward healing some of the fissures in my heart. I might not have a soulmate, a one-on-one partner to share my days, but I had more love surrounding me, holding me in its arms, than most people.

I was blessed.

So very blessed.

Nate had been taking the kids, including Elizabeth, every other weekend since my return from England. The arrangements had been made through our son—who also continued to deliver Nate's check.

I started going to a Methodist church down the road—mostly when the kids were gone, but they occasionally came with me. It felt good to spend an hour now and then fully focused on God. And I volunteered a lot. I had friends, mothers of my sons' friends, women from church, but no one I got too close to. I'd always been a private person. And that didn't change even now that I was on my own.

The boys told me, shortly after we came home from California, that Nate had asked them and Elizabeth to spend Christmas Eve with him. He promised to have them back by the time I returned from the candlelight service at church.

I would have them to myself on Christmas Day.

I ached at the thought of him spending the day alone—or even with someone else without his children. I had to remind myself that this situation was of his own making.

Nate had not only betrayed me, he'd betrayed himself. And he was paying the price.

On New Year's Day, my sons lamented when All American Iowa running back Ronnie Harmon fumbled the ball four times during his last game. I didn't care. I'd never been a football fan.

Neither had their father, but since entering high school the boys had developed an interest in the sport.

That same day, my all-time favorite singer, Barbra Streisand, ended her relationship with Jon Peters. I felt we were kindred spirits.

And Lori called. Wayne had flown to London for Christmas. He'd brought divorce papers for her to sign.

On January 2nd, 1986, just after Elizabeth went down for her nap, the phone rang and I grabbed it before it could wake her. "Hello?"

"Eliza?"

Six months, two weeks and three days, and still I knew his voice instantly.

"Nate?" My heart started to pound. "What's wrong?" Something had happened to one of the boys. I just knew it.

A broken leg, maybe. The boys were working at the resort during their winter vacation, and sometimes they hit the slopes on their lunch break. My keys were on the table by the front door. Elizabeth's parka was hanging on the hook above it.

"Nothing's wrong. The boys are fine."

He could still read my mind. There was some comfort in that.

And some pain, too.

"I had an offer on the resort." He named a well-known, moderately priced hotel chain. Gave me the amount. "What do you think?"

"It's a good offer." I focused on the question. Anything else hurt too much. "If you want to retire, or do something else, you should take it. If not, then don't. There can always be another offer."

Perhaps a bigger one.

But we didn't need the money. Even when we'd had far less, finances had never been a problem.

"That's what I thought, too. Thanks."

"You're welcome."

He hung up before I could ask him which he was going to do.

★ ★ ★

Nate kept the resort. I'd have found out soon enough if he hadn't. My name was on the title. But that night Keith told me his father had turned down the offer.

Both boys seemed relieved.

And I guess I was, too.

Two weeks later, Nate called again. Based on national test scores, Keith had been offered a full scholarship to a private boarding school in Denver the next fall for his final two years of high school. Over the weekend, he'd told his father about the recruiter who'd visited his school to make the offer.

I'd heard during a meeting with Keith and the private school's headmaster the previous week.

"I don't think he should go." Nate's stance was unusually adamant from the outset.

I wasn't sure I did, either. "Why not?"

"He'd advance academically, probably get a better chance at a university scholarship, but we can afford to pay his tuition. The most important lessons he's going to learn in high school aren't necessarily academic."

I didn't disagree. "I went to a private high school."

"You had specific goals that were very different from Keith's."

I'd reached the same conclusion.

"I don't want to deny him this chance because of some perception that I need him here," I said.

"You have to admit it's a help that he's been driving Jimmy around."

"Yes, and in a few years they're both going to be gone and I'll be back to driving around—with Elizabeth."

I ran my fingers through my hair. I'd been letting it grow. And had it streaked as a Christmas present to myself. I was now the proud bearer of blond highlights.

"It's convenient having Keith's help, but not imperative." I wanted that clear. "Besides, Jimmy'll have his license before Keith leaves."

"If he gets it as soon as his older brother did," Nate said. "I'm not so sure he's going to be ready."

Remembering an incident with Jimmy and an electric cart at the resort the week before, I wasn't so sure, either. Jimmy was more of a dreamer than practical like Keith.

"Keith and I have had several conversations about the scholarship," I said now, needing to focus on the task at hand before my thoughts carried me places I couldn't afford to go. "But I can't get a feel for what he really wants. Does he want to go because he'd like us to be proud of him? Because it's an honor to be asked? Is his hesitation to go because of me?"

"Maybe some of both."

"I really believe this should be his decision. I'll support him either way. I just want to be sure he's making it for the right reasons."

"I don't think he can, Liza." It was the first time he'd called me that since the day he left. "As mature as Keith is, he's still a kid, like most guys his age. He's trying to be responsible. And his head's being turned by the school's headmaster. I'm not sure he even *knows* what he wants."

"Maybe we should give him some time to think about it, then."

"He told me the offer expires at the end of the month."

"Maybe they'll give him more time. They seem to want him badly enough."

"I think now's the time you and I have to be parents and make the decision for him. Hell, Liza, he hasn't even been on a date yet. How's that ever going to happen if he's stuck away in an all boys' school?"

He had a point there. Though from the stories I'd heard, and the movies I'd seen, boys did manage to find a way.

Some boys. Probably not Keith.

"I also hate to see him and Jimmy split up," he said. "They're opposite enough that they're good for each other."

Their differences caused a lot of squabbles. But my sons were close, too.

I thought about all of that and finally said, "Okay."

"We're agreed then? He won't go?"

"Yes."

"Would you like to tell him or should I?"

I handled most of the kids' problems singlehandedly. "You can."

Nate said he'd talk to Keith the next time he saw him and rang off.

He didn't ask how I was. Or if I needed anything.

And I didn't ask him, either.

That was the way it was between us now.

"Jimmy said last night that Elizabeth counted to five this week."

"Nate?" I glanced at the clock. Six a.m. On Saturday morning—Nate's weekend with the kids. I'd stayed up half the night playing Atari games on television and drinking wine.

Feeling sorry for myself.

Thinking I had all day today to sleep it off.

It had been a couple of weeks since our last conversation about Keith's school.

"Did I wake you? You're always up early."

Not anymore. Not when I had to wake up alone. Spend the waking hours without my family.

"I'm awake." Lori had called the night before to tell me she'd met someone. We'd talked a long time. She was taking it slow, but found herself getting excited about life again.

She also told me her father hadn't so much as shaken another woman's hand since the day I'd kicked him out.

"The boys tried to make Elizabeth count again last night, but she wouldn't," he was saying, and I pulled my thoughts back.

My youngest child, four months shy of her third birthday, already had a very strong will.

"She can count to twenty," I told him. "She just hasn't done it for them yet so they think I'm making it up."

"She sang her ABC's last night. All the way through. Got *Q* and *W*, too."

I didn't know Nate was aware that those letters had stumped her. But I guess it made sense that he would be.

"Anyway," he said, "I was wondering if maybe we should put her in preschool."

That woke me up. "No."

"It would free you up some, Liza. Let you do things for you."

"Raising my child *is* doing for me. It's what I want to do. Besides, I'm a teacher, Nate, remember? I'm as qualified as anyone else to give her her best start."

"Still…"

"I'm not sending her to preschool. The boys didn't go."

"They had each other to play with."

"I really don't want to, Nate. I'd like to give her a couple more years of unstructured time, of learning her values from us."

"She needs socialization skills."

I wasn't sending her. Period. I'd divorce him first. And sue for complete custody. I'd move back to California and live with my mother. I'd—

"I have a compromise."

It occurred to me, when I heard his tone, that Nate Grady had just played me.

"What?"

"Bring her to the resort, to the toddler day care room, one or two days a week."

We'd established it shortly after buying the place as part of our intention to provide a full-service family establishment. The parents could ski while their kids were safely entertained.

"And what do you suggest I do while she's there?"

"Get your hair done. Volunteer at the shelter. Ski. Read a book. Check up on the special event staff—or any of the other staff. You own half the place. Do whatever you want."

Surprisingly, I felt a little thrill at the thought. I couldn't remember the last time I'd felt one.

Probably before Nate left.

"Okay, but if she's not happy, I'm pulling her out."

"You've got a deal."

I hung up, nervous about what I'd gotten myself into.

Chapter 14

In April of that year, Pope John Paul II met Rome's chief rabbi at the synagogue in Rome in a quest for peace. I was proud of the Church I'd once belonged to. And hopeful for the world.

I tried not to be quite so hopeful where Nate was concerned, but it was getting harder and harder. He was calling every week now. Always when the kids were either asleep or out.

Mostly that meant Elizabeth was asleep and Jimmy and Keith were out. The boys had found a group of friends to hang out with and were gone more often than they were home that spring. Jimmy had a girlfriend. Her name was Lindsay. He'd already told me he was going to marry her. Keith still hadn't been on a date.

"Give him time," Nate told me late one Friday night when I worried aloud about my eldest son.

The boys were both out—Jimmy on a double date at the midnight drive-in, and Keith with a couple of buddies at the races in Denver.

"I just hate the thought of him living his life alone." It felt too much like my own brokenhearted state.

"Keith's not going to be the type to jump from girl to girl." Nate's voice was tired, but peaceful-sounding. "Mark my words, when he meets the right one, that will be that."

"At least until it isn't." I regretted the words the moment I spoke them. Didn't want to challenge him. Or dig at him.

I didn't want any more bad feelings between us. We had children to raise.

"Unless it always is." Nate's soft reply was unexpected. And left me speechless.

The third week in April, after days and days of hype and media coverage, journalist Geraldo Rivera opened Al Capone's vault on live television and found…nothing. The man was an instant laughingstock in many circles, losing the trust of his readers and public.

Somehow Nate and I got into a discussion about the fiasco. He'd called to see if his sons were having dinner with him the following night—the beginning of his weekend with the kids—or only Elizabeth. When we'd sorted that out, he just hadn't hung up.

"He did it to himself," I told him. "He came on so strong, *guaranteeing* that there'd be something to see."

"He couldn't help it that there wasn't anything in that vault."

"Of course he couldn't. And, knowing that, he made promises, anyway. People believed him because they trusted him."

"Know what I think?" Nate's voice was soft.

Elizabeth had been in bed for over an hour. The boys were at a high school basketball play-off game in Denver. I'd come upstairs to take a bath and was sitting propped up on a pillow, still waiting to do that.

"What?" I finally asked. Because I discovered I really did want to know.

"I think *he* believed. And because his belief was so strong, it took on a power of its own."

"If that's true, then belief can be a very dangerous thing."

"But wouldn't it be better to believe, and find out you're wrong, than never to believe in anything?"

I probably wasn't the right person to ask. "He made promises without being able to follow through."

"So Geraldo should be hung out to dry for trying?"

"You think there shouldn't be consequences for misleading so many people?" Even though the cause itself—Capone's vault—was a trivial one, it was the principle that mattered here.

"Of course. And his reputation's taken a hit. But does the fact that he made a mistake preclude him from ever being forgiven? From being permitted to try again? To make amends?"

We weren't talking about Geraldo Rivera. Maybe we never had been.

"He was so convincing," I said slowly. "How would people ever be able to believe in him again?"

"I guess he'd have to rebuild their trust in him."

I wasn't at all sure that was possible.

"If his motive was purely selfish, with no care for the people whose trust he betrayed, then I'd say he doesn't have a shot in hell of ever regaining anyone's trust. Or deserving it."

The phone was slipping from my sweaty palm. I switched hands.

"What if he'd known he was going to hurt people and did it anyway?" I asked. "How could they possibly trust him after that?"

"His emotional need was a weakness that got the better of him, clouding his judgment. How do you know he wasn't scrambling, hoping to rectify his mistake before it became public?"

My chin was trembling, but I refused to give in to tears.

"What was his original goal, Nate? To be successful at all cost? Was he *really* thinking of others? Or just himself?" I had to talk about Geraldo. It was the only way I was going to get through this.

"Is life ever that black and white, Liza?"

I didn't have an answer. I wanted it to be. I knew that

much. Or at least, I wanted some things to be. The ones on which I'd built the foundation of my life.

"I think his goal was to serve the people who trusted him, yet satisfy himself at the same time," Nate said slowly. "That's the goal of any decent man. He doesn't set out to betray others."

The hardest part of all of this was that my heart was responding to it. I felt the rightness of what Nate was saying.

Just as I felt the hopelessness of trying to forget.

"But what if his...weakness overcomes him again?" I asked softly.

"He's learned the key lesson. The weakness wasn't his downfall."

"What was his downfall?" I had to ask.

"The fact that he was too ashamed of his weakness to admit it. So he hid it, and in hiding, it grew. And eventually he ended up with something even more shameful."

Oh, my God. I was sobbing. Too hard to think.

"Liza?"

He had to stop. To leave me alone.

"Are you okay, Liza?"

I opened my mouth to tell him not to call me again.

"Come home, Nate. Please?"

I hadn't moved since I'd hung up the phone. Never did get my bath. I just sat there, propped up by pillows in the dark, waiting.

Anticipating.

And fearing.

If he was ever unfaithful to me again, I'd never be able to trust *anyone,* because I wouldn't be able to trust my own heart. I'd become embittered and disillusioned.

Could I afford to take that chance?

Wouldn't it be better to continue raising our children in a semifriendly manner? We'd found a measure of peace, Nate and I. Wouldn't it be best to leave it at that?

I heard his key in the lock. And shivered. It was so long since I'd been touched.

I loved him so much.

He took the stairs two at a time. I counted. He didn't even pause at Elizabeth's bedroom door before he appeared in ours.

The look on Nate's face as he sought me out in the darkness was another thing I'd never forget. He was afraid.

Of me?

Of hoping?

I couldn't make sense of what I was doing. Couldn't justify any of it. I just did what I had to do. I held out my arms.

"Oh, God, Liza…" Nate's voice broke. He joined me on the bed, sliding his arms around me. He was trembling.

For a long time he just held on, his breathing erratic. And then he looked up at me, as though he had something to say.

But didn't know what. Or maybe how.

"Kiss me?" I'd been alone for almost a year, so begging seemed appropriate.

Groaning, Nate pushed me down against the covers. His mouth devoured mine with even more hunger than on our wedding night. I was a seasoned woman now, not a timid virgin, and he unleashed his hunger on me without restraint.

I welcomed his intensity, knowing it spoke of a need so deep he was no longer able to contain it. I knew because I felt exactly the same way.

A couple of hours later we lay against the pillows, a small light on Nate's nightstand the only illumination. I'd made some decaf coffee, put on a short silk robe I'd purchased for my birthday. Nate was wearing a pair of his son's basketball shorts.

Our shoulders were touching as we sat and sipped.

"Your hair's longer." Nate picked up a lock, ran it through his fingers.

"Yeah."

"I like it."

I warmed under his praise like a schoolgirl.

"The boys'll be home soon." They'd see their father's car in the drive. I smiled as I pictured their expressions.

"Do you want me to go?"

My heart froze. "Go?"

Nate frowned, his eyes filled with pain as he perused me. "I screwed up. Badly. And that means I forfeited my rights in this household. You call the shots here, Liza."

"So you're just going to leave me?" I was so shocked I couldn't understand what he was trying to say.

Had I made the biggest mistake of my life? Become a one-night stand for my estranged husband?

Surely there'd been… The way he'd touched me…loved me… My body was still tingling.

"I'm going to do whatever you need me to do."

I didn't want a doormat.

"What I need is for you to be honest. With me. And with yourself. And do whatever *you* need to do." The words came out with the force of my confusion. "I don't want you here as some…some act of contrition. Or out of pity."

His scrutiny was unnerving.

"You mean that?"

"Yes."

"You're sure?"

"Absolutely."

He jumped out of bed, setting his cup down on the stand, and reached for his clothes.

"You're leaving."

"I'm going to the resort to pack and as soon as it's light I'm renting a truck, unloading the storage bin I've been renting and moving my things back where they belong. Here. In my home. With my family."

Light-headed, having trouble breathing, I sat there staring as tears welled up in my eyes.

"Nate?"

He was buttoning his shirt and looked over at me. "Yeah?"

"You have two able-bodied sons who can help with

that tomorrow. Why don't you come back to bed now—to your bed—and get a few hours' rest so you can keep up with them."

His hands stilled.

"I'm not going to wake up in the morning and change my mind about you, Nate."

"You might."

"Really?" I lifted my chin to stare at him.

I smiled as his hands slowly unfastened the buttons and waited for him to shed the rest of his clothes. Then, setting down my own cup, I held back the covers.

"Come to bed, my love."

He did.

"And if you ever, *ever* think about leaving it—or me—again, I will be through with you until death and beyond."

I wasn't sure I'd be able to follow through on that threat, but I knew it needed to be said.

"I love you, Liza."

"I love you, too."

"I'm not perfect."

"Me, neither."

"But this I can swear to you. I'd sooner die than leave you, or this bed, again."

That was enough for me.

The next night, with all of Nate's belongings back in their rightful places, the five of us sat down to dinner together for the first time in over a year. We'd told the boys they needn't cancel their plans with friends in order to stay home, but they both insisted. Keith offered to grill the steaks. Jimmy wanted to mix drinks—was given an unequivocal no—and settled for keeping an eye on Elizabeth while Nate supervised Keith and I prepared the salad and potatoes.

And after dinner, as if by unspoken agreement, we all moved into the living room. Nate sat at the piano I'd seen him glance at several times that day, and started to play.

Four hours later we were still there. Elizabeth had been asleep for a long time. The boys had drifted off, kissing me goodnight on their way, and stopping to tell their dad they were glad he was home. And, with my heart floating, I laid my head back against my chair, knowing all was right with my world.

I recognized the chord instantly. Started to smile.

And was still smiling through my tears as Nate finished the last chorus of "My Cup Runneth Over."

Mine did, too.

We threw a huge party at the resort for Elizabeth's third birthday. Keith and Jimmy invited their friends, who all came. My mom and sisters Bonnie, Alice and June flew in with their families. William, too. Most of our off-duty staff was there. Nate acted like a besotted schoolboy, never leaving my side, and I reveled in his attention. Elizabeth might have received all the presents that day, but Nate and I knew the real celebration was less for our sunny three-year-old than for the family that was once again whole.

Lori was the only one missing but she called. With good news of her own. She and her new beau, Charles, were getting married. We tried to talk her into a wedding this time around, but she said at thirty-two, she just wanted to tie the knot and settle down to babymaking. They were taking a Mediterranean cruise, getting married aboard ship, and would be home at Christmas so everyone could meet Charles.

Her parents, Holly and Todd, were flying out to cruise with them.

Nate seemed at peace with the news.

Our lives were completely blessed.

Elizabeth turned four and our world continued to evolve. Keith was eighteen that summer—old enough to vote. And at thirty-seven, I still felt as though I had more to figure out than I'd already learned. And we finally let Jimmy get his driver's license.

Both boys, along with their father, spent many hours on the ski slopes that winter. And at Christmastime, when Lori and Charles came for what we hoped was becoming an annual visit, I allowed Elizabeth to put on her first pair of baby skis.

That was it, though. I couldn't tolerate the idea of her on the slopes quite yet.

We had many evenings around the piano during their week-long visit, chatting, playing cards while Nate serenaded us, or engaging in rousing singalongs.

Lori still wasn't pregnant and we had long talks about

life and its vagaries and finding happiness in spite of them.

When it was time for her to leave, I was very sad to see them go. London was so far away and it looked as though they were going to make England their permanent residence.

Elizabeth loved playing with the other kids at the resort and by the spring of 1988, I started back to work there part-time. Elizabeth would be five soon, and entering kindergarten that fall. The same time Keith left for college…

I figured I'd plan ahead and find myself something to do to take the sting out of the passing years—and our changing lives. I signed up to volunteer at the battered women's shelter again. Two days a week this time. It felt right.

I alternately wept and smiled through my eldest son's high school graduation, with Nate standing beside me, holding my hand. And Elizabeth squirming to see.

"Where is he, Mama?" She must have asked at least fifteen times.

I'm not sure she ever picked him out in the crowd of two hundred. She was too busy stringing the buttons we'd brought along to keep her occupied. Over the needle, down the string went hundreds of tiny buttons, only to come off and be restrung in a different order.

Maybe she'd grow up to be a fashion designer.

I could think of worse things.

And better ones, too.
Mostly I just wanted my children to be happy.
As happy as I was.

Chapter 15

Nate took Elizabeth and me to Hawaii in late August of 1988. We left the day after Keith went off to college. My oldest child was the age I'd been when I'd met and married Nate.

Jimmy, 18 now and entering his senior year of high school, was working—and living—at the resort while we were in Hawaii. He'd been invited to go with us, but hadn't wanted to leave Jenny, his girlfriend of the moment. She was his ninth "serious" love.

"I worry about that boy," I told Nate one morning as we strolled along the sandy Maui beach outside the condo we'd rented. Elizabeth was making paper leis at the kids' club in the resort's main lodge. "He dives head-first into every relationship and ends up hurt."

"Give him time," my sage husband said, sliding his arm around me and pulling me close. It was more than two years after he'd come home, and I still thrilled at his attention. "Jimmy's just finding his way," he added.

I hoped so. And fretted anyway.

"Look at your sister June's boy," Nate went on. "He dated at least fifteen girls before he met Samantha. And they've been married, what, seven years now?"

I nodded. They had two darling little girls and lived in Texas. I'd only seen pictures of them, but my mother kept me informed.

"Jimmy's going to college next year," I reminded Nate. "What if he trades majors like he does girls?" We could be paying for college straight through the next decade.

"I don't think he will." The tide came in, soaking our feet. "He's been adamant all along about wanting to major in English and teach high school. That doesn't seem to waver."

"I guess."

But it was a mother's job to be concerned about her children.

Even after they were grown and gone.

"There's a message for you, Mrs. Grady," the plump, dark-haired woman said as we walked through the lobby of the resort a few minutes later. "It sounded urgent. I put it through to your phone."

With my heart pounding and Nate's hand tightly

clamped in mine, I rode the elevator up to our two-bedroom unit that overlooked the ocean.

The message light on the phone was blinking.

I recognized William's voice and went cold. Listened. And then, carefully replacing the receiver, sank down onto the bed.

"What is it?" Nate was there beside me, his hand at my back. "Liza?"

"Mom was in a head-on collision. A young girl was passing in a no-pass zone. Mom never knew what hit her."

"When?"

"This morning. She was on her way to bingo." I felt his warmth next to me. And that was all I felt. Except a headache. Like my skull was swelling and filling with air.

"How bad is it?"

I shook my head, fumbled with my hands in my lap. "She—" Glancing up at him, I started coming apart. "She died, Nate."

I needed him to do something about that. To make it all better.

"Oh, my God."

Both of his arms came around me, cradling me. "I'm so sorry, baby. So sorry." His face was pressed to the top of my head as he held me. Kissed me.

I have no idea how long I sat there, but I know time passed in that Hawaii resort suite because the sun rose higher, the maid came to clean and then went away. And all the while, as fear and loss attacked me, ravaged me, Nate was there, holding on.

"I don't know how to live without her." I'd cried all the tears I had. Now there were only words. And pain. "I've never spent one day on this earth without her."

"I know."

Pulling away only enough to look at him, I said, "I just can't believe it."

"You need to talk to William. Find out what the plans are. I'll call down and have them keep Elizabeth a little longer while I make arrangements to get us to California."

I nodded, but clutched at him as he started to move away. "Don't go."

Nate nodded. And stayed by my side as I called my brother, cried with him and told him we'd get home as soon as we could. William, Mom's executor, wanted all of us there before he did anything. June and Alice were already with him. Bonnie and her husband were driving up from San Diego that afternoon.

And Nate kept a hand on my thigh, or an arm against mine, as he got us on the first flight out of Maui. We'd be in San Francisco by dinnertime. Keith and Jimmy were going to meet us there.

My mother's death changed something inside me. I think that in the months following her funeral, I finally grew up. Until that point, a part of me had always been her little girl. I couldn't fall back on her anymore.

And maybe that was why, when Elizabeth started

school a couple of weeks later, I dropped her off, dry-eyed. I drove to the resort and went to work. Something had become very clear to me. Life was filled with change.

Changes were good as well as bad, and there was no way to stop them from coming. They *were* life. I could either live my life. Or not.

I wanted to live.

My new awareness of the total lack of control I felt over most of the things my heart relied on brought its own kind of peace.

Acceptance, Nate called it. I remembered him telling me—the night after we met—that my sense of acceptance was something he wanted. Was it something I'd had all along? And just forgotten?

Or maybe as a nineteen-year-old entering the convent I'd simply had less to lose? No husband, no children…

In any event, it saw me through Jimmy's graduation the following spring. His departure for college. And Elizabeth's going into first grade. I can't say I didn't feel intense pangs during every one of those major occurrences, but I weathered them.

Both boys had elected to attend Colorado State University in Fort Collins, rather than the University of Colorado right there in Boulder. They'd also decided to room together, which made me feel better about sending Jimmy off.

The movie *Dead Poet's Society* with Robin Williams came out that summer and Jimmy, having seen it repeatedly, was more certain than ever that he was going to be a high school English teacher—at an all-boys' high school.

Nate wasn't as pleased as I was, but he didn't dissuade our son from his goals. Rather, when the boys were home for Christmas break, Nate took Jimmy to Denver to visit a couple of all-boys' high schools and to speak with the headmasters.

Lori and Charles came for Christmas again that year. And on the first night, while the guys were all downstairs watching a movie on the new large-screen television set, I came out of Elizabeth's room to find my stepdaughter waiting for me.

"Can we talk?"

"Of course." I led her to the room I shared with her father and patted the bed. "Have a seat."

Out of habit, I settled on my side, piling the pillows behind my back, and Lori did the same with Nate's.

"What's up?"

"Charles and I have been having tests. Fertility stuff."

"And?"

I knew it wasn't good when her eyes filled with tears. "Turns out I'm infertile."

"Oh, honey." I covered her hand with mine. "I'm so sorry."

"Yeah," she sniffed, looking down at our interlocked hands. "Me, too."

"Is there anything they can do? New medical procedures are being discovered all the time and—"

Lori shook her head. "My ovaries don't produce eggs. We've tried hormones and other things, but it's just not going to happen."

"What does Charles say?"

"That we can adopt."

I nodded. "There are a lot of great kids out there who need to be loved."

"Yeah, I just... I don't know...."

I saw those eyes, so like her father's, shadowed with pain, and brushed the hair back from Lori's shoulder. "You're only thirty-four. You've got time to think about it."

"That's what Charles says. I was so set on having kids of my own, you know. And now that I can't, I'm starting to wonder if maybe I just wasn't meant to be a mother."

"You're meant to be whatever your heart tells you to be."

This was the one thing I stood by. Period. The one law by which my life had been lived. Through all its ups and downs.

And it had served me well.

Lori's eyes searched mine. "And if I decide I'd rather spend my life alone with Charles? Traveling, studying, working...would that make me less of a woman?"

"Of course not."

She licked her lips. "Would you think any less of me?"

"No!"

"You're the consummate mother, Eliza. You make motherhood look like the crowning glory of life."

"Because I fell in love with your father, married him

and got pregnant. Life chose it for me more than I chose it for myself."

"Are you sorry about any of it?"

I didn't answer right away. Not because I felt any uncertainty, but because I wanted to take the time to reflect, to give Lori, and myself, the complete truth.

"I'm sorry I lost Sarah. Had I known how horrible that would be, I might not have had the courage to marry your father. And I'm sorry about our separation. But truthfully? When I consider everything life has given me, with him, and with our children—no, I don't have the slightest regret."

Lori contemplated that—or something else, I don't know. I gave her time. And then I said, "You're a gifted attorney, my dear. And a wonderful wife to a man who has a lot of interests, a lot of professional goals. A man who wants you to share in all of those. If the two of you also want to share the raising of a child, then you'll know it. But, please—" I looked her straight in the eye "—don't even consider doing that out of some sense of guilt or obligation. The only dishonorable thing you can do with your life is to live it in a way that's contrary to your heart."

Lori watched me for another few seconds, and then smiled. A tentative expression, but positive nonetheless.

"What do you say we go downstairs, pour ourselves a glass of wine and find some good recipes for Christmas dinner?" I suggested.

"Sounds great."

I got up, straightened the pillows and met Lori at the door.

"Thank you," she said.

"You don't have to thank me." I gave her a hug—and held on. "You're the one who welcomed me all those years ago when you came looking for your father and accepted me, too. You have no idea how much that meant to me."

"Not nearly as much as it means to me now."

I kissed her cheek, took her hand and walked downstairs with her. I might be losing some of the things I'd held dear in my thirties—kids home every day, all activities, even diapers. But I was gaining, too.

Whatever life might bring me, I knew that Lori would always be part of it. Part of Nate's life and part of mine. We were bound together in love and support. There was nothing I wanted more than that.

After all, wasn't that what my life had been about since the moment he'd walked into that bar twenty-one years before and took command of my heart?

I missed my mother horribly that Christmas. The family gathered around to watch the *I Love Lucy* Christmas special, aired for the first time in thirty years, and I remembered when, as a little girl, I'd sit with my mom and dad and laugh at Lucy's antics on our old black-and-white television.

Elizabeth was more interested in having a tea party with her Cabbage Patch doll and talked her father into joining her. He sat in one of the two child-size chairs at the activity table we'd set up for her in the living room.

I cried only a little when the boys went back to school. Lori and Charles had returned to London the week before and the house was quieter than I liked.

But before she'd left, Lori had given me an idea. Family law was her specialty and she'd spent a lot of time telling me about some of the women and children she'd represented—victims of domestic violence. Women like the ones at the shelter where I volunteered in whatever capacity they needed me. Sometimes cooking or running errands, sometimes playing with the kids. She'd said a dose of me was just what these women needed. In a more active capacity.

According to her, I was an example of what could be.

I couldn't get her statements out of my mind during the months that followed. When I got involved in other things, something outside myself would bring those comments back. A television show. An article I was reading. Some remark I'd hear someone make.

And as New York City saw the swearing-in of its first black mayor, as my daughter grew more adamant that she was right and I was wrong—about everything—and my sons opted to stay in Fort Collins and work for the summer, I began to seriously consider another life change.

Just to be sure, I spent less time working at the resort that summer and volunteered more often at the battered women's shelter. I spent my time out of the kitchen and with the women themselves.

"Keith called me at work today," Nate said one night

in late August. We were lying naked beneath the sheet, having just made love.

"What about? Are they coming home for the weekend?"

Classes were due to start the next week.

"No."

I was, of course, disappointed. I still had a hard time not taking it personally when my sons didn't need to see me as much as I needed to see them. But I'd learned to be pretty good at not letting on how desperately I craved their visits.

"He wanted to talk about two things. First, he let me know that Jimmy and Rhonda broke up."

We'd met the girl the previous spring, when Jimmy had brought her home for a weekend visit. I'd liked her as well as all his other female friends.

I nodded. "And the second thing?"

"He asked me what I thought about him switching his major to hotel management. He'd like to work for me full-time when he graduates and someday take over the resort."

Nate sounded surprised. I wasn't at all.

"What'd you tell him?"

"That I had to talk to you first regarding the resort, but that he had my full support on the major if he's sure it's what he wants to do. I need to know he's not doing this because he feels he owes us."

"Keith loves the resort. He was miserable in Fort Collins this summer."

"He never said anything to me about that."

"It probably isn't the kind of thing a guy talks to his dad about." I couldn't help the cocky little note in my voice.

Leaning over, Nate nipped lightly at my lips with his teeth. "Then I guess it's just as well he's got a mama, isn't it?"

I couldn't agree more. And spent the next half hour rewarding Nate for being so astute.

"Speaking of the resort, I have something I want to run by you," I said the next morning over breakfast. Elizabeth had spent the night with a friend she'd met in first grade who was also going to be in her second-grade class when school resumed after Labor Day.

Nate looked up from the paper and grinned at me. "Were we speaking of the resort?"

"Uh-huh." I couldn't eat the toast I'd made for myself. My stomach had been invaded by butterflies. "Last night. About Keith."

"Oh, right. So what about it?"

Putting the paper down, he gave me his full attention. Which made me even more nervous. For once, I had no idea what kind of reaction I was going to get.

"Well, this doesn't have anything to do with Keith, actually—though you are going to call him today, aren't you? And tell him that Jimmy and Elizabeth will be given the same opportunity but we'd love to have him in the business?"

"Is that what we'd love?"

I blinked. "Wouldn't you? Over the years, you've

given so much of yourself to the place, taken it from something mediocre to an impressive venture with a niche all its own."

"We could sell it and be set for life."

"We *are* set for life. Besides, what would we do with all the extra money except leave it to the kids?"

"If we don't sell, it'll always be a part of our lives. Even when I retire and quit going in every day, Keith will still call with questions. He'll still run things by me."

"Is that bad?"

He shook his head, the lines around his eyes crinkling as he grinned. "No, I think that sounds pretty damn good. I just wanted to make sure you knew what we'd be getting into. We'll be signing on for life."

"Haven't we already done that?"

I wasn't speaking just of the resort, but it applied. That business was a part of our family, just like our house and our piano and our memories.

"I'll call him this morning."

I smiled, and sipped my coffee. Our son would graduate. And he would come home. Oh, not to live under my roof, I knew that. But to take his place in a life that Nate and I had built. The thought made me feel cozy. Secure.

Sometimes things worked out just the way you hoped.

"You never told me what you wanted to talk about— something to do with the resort."

I'd realized that, of course, but I'd decided I'd ponder

things a little longer, enjoy the anticipation before I risked the possibility that Nate might not be as excited by my plan as I was.

Glancing at him over my shoulder, I left the water running in the sink, rinsing our coffee cups for the dishwasher. I saw that Nate had his briefcase in one hand.

"We can talk about it tonight."

He set his briefcase on the table. "How about if we do it right now?"

He'd figured out it was important to me. I should've known.

Perhaps I *had* known. From the moment I'd broached the subject that morning. Nate understood me.

I turned off the water. Dried my hands. And faced him. "What would you think about me quitting work?"

"That'd be fine. You don't have to work. You know that." He was frowning. "I'm just not sure it'd be good for you to stay at home all day."

"Me, neither." I'd get too lonely. And feel worthless. "We know me too well, huh?"

"So I take it you have something else in mind?"

"I've been spending more time at the women's shelter in Denver. In addition to my regular volunteer days, I've been going when I drop Elizabeth off at the dance studio and help the women while she's in class."

"Help them how?"

"Write letters, do their hair, play with their children." Hands clasped behind my back, I waited.

"Why didn't you say anything about it?"

"I don't know. I guess I needed to feel things out for myself before I could talk about it. I wasn't convinced I'd like it. Or be good at it."

When he nodded, his expression contemplative, I told him about my talks with Lori. And all the times his daughter's words had come back to me over the past months.

"I feel I need to do something with this, Nate."

"Then I'm sure you should."

I told him about my eventual plan to open a shelter in Boulder. Not a government-run one like the one in Denver, but a private one, where I'd have less red tape to deal with and more control over the rules. I'd need funding, though. We talked it over and decided I'd spend a few years in some official capacity at the shelter in Denver first and then see where my heart led me.

Chapter 16

In the spring of 1991, just before her eighth birthday, my second-grade daughter came home from school to announce that she was quitting dance class. She didn't like it. And she wanted to play soccer. So I became a soccer mom.

I was forty-two years old, standing on the sidelines with women ten years my junior, cheering for the only girl on the team. Nate made it to every game that spring and during the '91-'92 season, became the coach of Elizabeth's team.

Some things don't take much training—only heart.

Keith graduated from Colorado State University with honors and a bachelor degree in hotel management.

And Jimmy introduced us to Lydia, the woman he was sure he was going to marry, and decided to spend his last college summer in Fort Collins so he could be close to her.

We'd missed Lori and Charles the previous Christmas. They'd been on a trip to Africa but were talking about getting to Colorado sometime that summer. I hoped they did. I was ready to approach the city of Boulder with my plan to open a battered women's shelter in a space I'd found a couple of miles from downtown. Even though Nate and I had written the plan and been over it many times, I wanted Lori's opinion before I presented it. She might have suggestions about agencies I should contact— dealing with government red tape was a natural for her after practicing law in Washington. And while I was going to have a private facility, I still needed to abide by certain regulations.

Elizabeth would be starting fourth grade that next fall; she was pulling away from me much more rapidly than her brothers had. As much as I worshipped the ground that girl walked on, she tried my patience.

Besides, at forty-three, I wasn't getting any younger.

We bought our first computer that summer. Keith said we needed a system for the resort if we were going to move into the twenty-first century with any success.

And Nate brought one home, as well. Elizabeth loved it and I had to fight to get her to help around the house— even just to keep her room picked up and to practice the piano. If she wasn't on the computer or playing with friends, she wanted to be at the resort with Keith.

Her big brother had a lot more patience with her than I did. And he was living in a suite at the resort, so she always had a place to hang out where she'd be safe and not in the way.

Lori didn't make it home, after all, but we wrote each other often, and the day after school started in September, I made an offer on the big, old house I'd picked out. With renovations I could get a common room, a kitchen, two dormitory-style bathrooms, and at least ten small bedrooms, each with enough room for a single bed and a set of bunks.

I hired a construction crew for the major carpentry, plumbing and electrical jobs, and Nate helped me work on the place every weekend that fall. By the new year, I was ready to interview counselors, a cook and house mothers. My licenses had come through, and so had some extra funding from the city. The resort was putting all its charitable contributions behind the venture, as well.

I was forty-two and just starting out.

The television series *Cheers* broadcast its last episode in May of 1993. Nate and I had been catching the show since it began, shortly after the end of our separation. I'd been fond of Sam Malone, bar owner, in spite of himself and was sad to see him go. Nothing, not even make-believe, lasted forever. Except maybe in reruns—and memories.

Jimmy graduated right on schedule, certified to

teach high school English, and already had a job at one of the schools he'd visited in Denver a few years before. He'd talked Sherry, the current woman of his dreams, into a position at a nearby parochial school. I was glad to hear she'd be living with her parents, who were from Denver, and not with him. Times had changed, but in that area, I had not.

On her tenth birthday, Elizabeth wandered down to the kitchen just as I was putting the finishing touches on her cake. Scraping frosting from the side of the bowl with her finger, she sneaked a taste.

"Hey," she said. "It's good."

As if she hadn't expected it to be? I raised my eyebrows in exaggerated disapproval.

And that night at the dinner table, with both of her brothers present, Jimmy with Sherry at his side, she cleared her throat and stood on her chair to make an announcement. She told everyone, but mostly her father and me, that beginning immediately, she was changing her name.

"I will no longer be answering to Elizabeth," she stated, her manner unequivocal as she stood there in jeans and a T-shirt, her arms folded across her chest. "From now on I'm Beth, so I'm my own person and not like my mother, Eliza."

It hurt. A lot. But I pretended not to notice. I was sure she meant in name only.

Beth was the one who told me that Keith had a steady girlfriend. I knew he'd dated occasionally, but never the same girl more than once or twice. Unlike his brother, he'd certainly never brought a girl home. Beth spent a lot of time at the resort during the summer of '93—whenever I was at the shelter, where I oversaw all the books and made executive decisions but left the women and children to the professionals who could help them. One day when I picked her up, she was full of the juicy news that she'd wheedled out of the house-keeping staff.

Keith had been seeing one of the maids. She was twenty.

"Four years younger than him, Mom," Beth said, her skinny legs bouncing on the seat as I drove. She'd grown in the two months since I'd bought her those shorts for her birthday. They were too small. "She has blond hair and she's working for the summer so she can afford to go back to UC in August. She's studying nutrition. Her dad's a minister and it's just the two of them."

"What happened to her mother?" I asked, ashamed of myself for prying. My son did not deserve a nosy mother who invited thirdhand gossip through a ten-year-old.

"Dunno. But it's cool that he's a minister, huh? Kinda like you entering the convent."

I could follow the logic—we'd both dedicated our lives to the service of God through organized religion—only his dedication had lasted. "Kind of."

"They've gone on dates every weekend since May, and Ethel says neither one of 'em's seeing anyone else."

Ethel. An older woman who'd been with us as long as we'd owned the resort.

"Have you met her?"

She grinned. "I talked to her a couple times, but she doesn't know that *I* know she's Keith's girlfriend."

"Does she know you're his sister?"

"I guess so. Doesn't everybody?"

"Does she have a name?" I figured if I was going to commit the offense, I might as well go all out.

"Uh-huh. Emily."

"Is she pretty?"

"'Course. She's with Keith!"

I wondered if my oldest son was using condoms. But I certainly didn't ask his busybody sister.

"Did you know Keith's seeing a girl in housekeeping?" I asked Nate as we lay in bed that night.

"No."

"He hasn't said anything to you about it?"

"No." He sounded half-asleep. We both had to be up early in the morning.

"Has he mentioned dating anyone at all?"

"No."

Nate rolled onto his back, laughing at me in the darkness. "You jealous?"

"Of what?"

"The fact that your oldest baby might be changing his loyalties from you to another woman?"

"Of course not!" The thought had never crossed my mind. At least, I didn't think it had.

"It just bothers me that he hasn't even mentioned her. I mean, I'm his mother."

"And he used to tell you everything."

Oh, hell. Nate was right. Again.

I *was* jealous. There'd been no threat with Jimmy. He'd had so many girlfriends there'd been no opportunity for a switch in allegiance. But Keith...

"He'll tell us when he's ready."

I wondered when that would be.

The older I got, the more confusing life became. I'd given up control years before, but my need for it still got the better of me now and then.

I was forty-five years old and sometimes I just didn't understand life. My perspective was clouded, I know, by the women and children I saw going in and out of the shelter. It was hard to reconcile myself to the untenable situations from which they'd come, the horror stories they had to tell, especially when I felt helpless to do anything about them. The shelter offered a great service. It couldn't fix the world.

But that didn't stop me from trying. To that end, in the spring of 1994, with Lori's long-distance help, I contacted all the local law firms in Boulder, as well as the college of law at UC, asking for volunteers to offer free legal advice to the women at the shelter.

"It's incredible," I told Nate over a meat-loaf-and-baked-potato dinner one night. "I was hoping for three or four responses—you know, thinking we'd do one night a month or something. As it turns out, I've got so many lawyers offering to help, including Roger Kempton, that defense attorney who handles so many of Denver's high-profile cases, that we'll be able to do two sessions a week."

Nate picked up a roll. Broke it and arranged a pat of butter in the middle, just like he'd been doing for the twenty-six years I'd known him. "Might be good if you could do one night and one day," he said. "That way women who work in the evenings can still get help."

"And private lawyers could do the day hours," I added. I'd started out thinking only government attorneys would be volunteering and they were committed during the day.

"Mom, can I have the other half of your potato? Coach says I need the carbs."

"Of course." Passing the foil-wrapped potato from my plate to hers, I got up and sliced the cake I'd made for dessert while Nate, who was no longer coaching now that Beth was on an all-star city team, discussed defensive strategy with his daughter.

We had a soccer game that night. I'd completely forgotten.

A week later, I asked Keith to bring his girlfriend to Beth's eleventh birthday dinner. We were going to her favorite restaurant on the 16th Street Mall in downtown Denver.

Ten months after I'd first heard about her, my son still hadn't mentioned this girl to me.

"That's okay, Mom. It's Beth's big day. She doesn't need a bunch of strangers hanging around."

What struck me was that he hadn't denied the girl's existence.

"Who is she?"

"Nobody."

He was sitting behind his desk at the resort. I'd stopped by to have lunch with Nate.

"I wonder how she'd feel if she could hear you refer to her like that?"

He had the grace to look ashamed. "Let it go, Mom, huh?"

I agreed. What else could I do?

But I didn't like it.

I asked Nate about her over lunch.

"He's never said a word to me."

"Have you met her?" She'd only worked at the resort for a couple of months the previous summer. I'd learned that from Beth.

"Don't you think I would've told you if I had?"

"Yeah."

"He's playing this one close to his chest, Liza. You just have to leave it alone."

I was pretty sure I couldn't. I'd tried.

"Doesn't it bother you?"

He shrugged, his eyes a little tired-looking as he glanced up at me. "I can't imagine telling my mom about the girls I dated. It's not something a guy usually wants to discuss with his mom."

"Jimmy does." He and Sherry had split. Brenda had been next. Now it was Kaylee.

"Because with him, it's never gone very deep."

That bothered me, too. I was worried about both boys.

"So you think he's serious about this girl?"

"This is Keith we're talking about. What do *you* think?"

Keith didn't do anything lightly or without reason. Kind of like his mother, Nate had said more than once. But a person had to be prepared.

"Is she going to be working here this next summer?"

"Not so far." Nate didn't seem concerned one way or the other.

I couldn't share his complacency.

Depending on just how serious my son was, the girl could become part of my immediate family. And I'd never even met her.

I longed for the days when I was in control of every bite the kid put in his mouth and knew every single time he went to the bathroom.

The summer of '94 brought another challenge my way. I was in the common room at the shelter, supervising a man who was installing a more intricate security system—one that would go off at the first sign of movement anywhere near the windows—when the front door opened. The security man and I were the only two people in the room. Our current residents were all having lunch.

A woman wearing sunglasses peeked inside but didn't enter.

"Come in," I said to her, leaving the technician to his job. I opened the door farther.

She looked over her shoulder, then quickly stepped inside, moving out of view of the still-open door. She was a pretty woman—in her early thirties, I guessed, and probably Hispanic. She was also, in midsummer, wearing a long-sleeved turtleneck shirt with a pair of lightweight cotton slacks.

"I've only got a minute," she said, speaking perfect English. "My sons are playing T-ball and I don't want to leave them for long."

"What can we do for you?"

I had two counselors on staff that day. And a house-mother who, just at the moment, was having her lunch.

The woman shrugged, her sunglasses still perched on the bridge of her nose. "I heard about this place last week and I've been thinking about it ever since. I wanted to stop by."

Our address wasn't common knowledge. It had to be that way to protect those we served. Usually women found us via referrals—through a hospital emergency room, more often than not. Or the police station when doctors reported suspected abuse.

"I'm Eliza Grady," I said, holding out a hand.

"Nice to meet you." The woman took my hand,

gave it a steady shake. I thought the top of her hand was bruised, but couldn't tell for sure. She didn't tell me her name. She was looking around and I couldn't tell if she liked what she saw or not.

I just knew she'd been led to me and I wanted to help her.

If I could.

"Would you like to come to my office?"

"Maybe for a minute."

I ushered her to the small room that served as my office before she could change her mind. Offered her a cup of coffee, which she refused. She was slim, a bit taller than my five foot five.

"This is a private facility and I'm the owner." I said the words that came to me. "There are professionals on staff who can assist you with just about any problem you might have. There's no charge for our services, but we do ask for donations if you're ever in a position to help us."

The woman's nod was jerky. But she said nothing, and, by her own admission, we had little time.

"Would you like me to get one of the counselors to speak with you?"

"No." Wringing her hands, she raised her head. And then removed her sunglasses. As I'd suspected, they'd been hiding a black eye. The fist-size bruise was still blood-red in parts. This wasn't an old injury.

"Who did that to you?"

"Doesn't matter."

"Of course it matters."

"Listen, I don't think you can help me. I don't think anyone can, but...um...I was wondering if I could tell you some things—confidentially—just in case...."

"Of course. Whatever you say won't leave this room. Unless you authorize me to take it elsewhere."

She nodded. Glanced at her watch and frowned. "My youngest guy is only four. He gets upset if I'm away from him for very long."

I smiled, remembering when my own sons were little.

"My name is Maria. My husband's name is Robert. We've been living in the States for seven years. Robert's a mechanic and has been at the same job ever since we came here. He makes good money. And...I'm pregnant."

I nodded. Waiting. That perfect little story wouldn't have brought her to me. It also didn't explain the bruises I could see—or the ones I couldn't but suspected were there. Ninety-degree weather didn't usually call for long-sleeved shirts.

"Robert came here with the help of his older brother. That's how he got his green card. Juan runs guns. And probably drugs, too. Because it's his brother, Robert sometimes helps him."

"Did Juan give you those bruises?"

She seemed about ready to nod, but at the last second shook her head. "Robert did that." The words were bitter. "He doesn't get mad often, but when he does, he's got a horrible temper."

I sat forward, possible solutions already tumbling through my mind. "How long has he been hitting you?"

"About five years."

A few years ago that might have shocked me.

"I'm used to it." She winced as she shrugged. "But last night, he threatened to hit our oldest boy."

I swallowed. Maintained calm when my stomach was roiling.

"We have a room available right now," I told her. "It's got a twin and a set of bunk beds. You and your sons are welcome to it."

For a moment it seemed as though hope passed through her expression. Then her face fell.

"Robert and I are not legally married," she said. "I mean, to us, we're husband and wife, but technically we aren't."

"That should make it easier for you to get away from him."

She shook her head, and I decided to let her finish before I said another word.

"You don't understand," she said. "Robert is here legally. I'm not. He's the father of American-born children. He's got a job—an income. I do not. If I leave, he'll get the kids and I'll get deported."

I was out of my league.

But a name came instantly to mind.

"I know someone who might be able to help," I told her. "If you'll give me your permission to talk to this person—no names, I promise—and then come back here tomorrow, I'll see if there's anything we can do."

"I don't have any money."

"I understand that." That was a concern I *could* handle for her. "It won't cost you anything."

Maria stood. "You promise no names?"

I did. And with a tentative smile, accompanied by a frightened nod, she hurried away.

Chapter 17

As soon as Maria left, I tried to call Nate. Her story had left me shaken. I was desperately afraid I wouldn't be able to help her. I needed his reassurance—and advice.

He didn't pick up.

I didn't have any time to waste.

I looked up a number, dialed and waited, hoping that I was doing the right thing.

"Roger Kempton, please," I said to the receptionist who answered.

"May I tell him who's calling?"

"Eliza Grady."

"One moment, please."

I was sure she'd come back and ask to take a message. Roger had much bigger fish to fry than me. A high-powered defense attorney and partner at one of the most prestigious firms in Boulder, he couldn't be expected to give priority to philanthropic activities.

"Eliza? Good to hear from you! Everything okay?"

I heaved a small sigh of relief. He'd taken my call. "Yes, of course, Roger. How are you?"

"Fine. Busy as usual. What's up?"

I explained my predicament. Apologized for calling on him like this, and asked if he had any advice I could give the woman. Knew of anyplace I could send her for legal counsel.

"I'll need to meet with her before I can give you any answers," he finally said. "I'm just looking at my calendar. Could we meet someplace outside the city the day after tomorrow? Around noon?"

"I don't know, but I'd guess so. This guy works during the day. She'd probably have to bring her kids."

"That's not a problem. I'd like you to be there, Eliza. She'll feel more comfortable."

"Roger, I never intended you to take this on yourself. You already give some of your very valuable time to the shelter."

"I want to do it." His voice was quiet. Serious. So I didn't question him further. "But be warned, I might not get anywhere with this."

I'd expected that.

"There are a lot of questions here and I'll need to

research case law, but I should get some specifics from her first."

"What are her chances? Do you have any idea?"

"I honestly don't know, Eliza." Every time he said my name, his voice was warm, almost like a caress. I'd never noticed that before. But then, I was pretty susceptible today. I was probably imagining things. "I'll get one of my clerks to do some case research. I can only promise you I'll do anything I can…."

At that moment, I could've hugged him.

I had the same thought two days later when—after he'd spent half an hour putting Maria at ease—he'd agreed to help her. Gratis. The first step was to move her from her trailer outside town to the shelter.

I asked Nate to help with that and he readily agreed. Keith came, too, and I was glad to have my husky son shadowing the slim woman as she moved quickly about her home, gathering essentials and a few of her children's favorite toys. Within an hour, we had Maria and her two boys safely ensconced in my last available room.

Roger called the next day. And the next. There were some things he wanted to discuss with me before he spoke to Maria, he said, asking if I could meet him for a cup of coffee midafternoon. I did. Without hesitation.

He was waiting for me at a coffeeshop near the campus. Because it was summer, the place was nearly deserted. He'd chosen a booth in the far back corner.

I would've thought one of the tables more appropriate, but was so thankful for his help, I didn't question his choice.

"Slide in over here," he said, moving next to the wall and patting the bench beside him. "I have a contract to show you."

Seeing the tiny print on the long form, I sat down as he asked, careful to keep a distance between us. Or as much of one as I could.

He put the contract down, sliding closer to me as he did so.

And I remembered his voice saying my name the other day. His willingness to help a woman he'd never met, without any hope of reimbursement.

I thought of Nate, with his graying hair, life-weathered face and agile body. He was busy at the resort, probably in the middle of an afternoon climb with a group of rowdy boys.

"This is an immigration contract," Roger said. And spent the next few minutes going over the concerns it raised. All things he could've told me over the phone.

None of which needed to be discussed with me before he talked to Maria. Or at all.

When he crossed his arm over mine while pointing out a particular phrase, grazing my breast with his elbow, I didn't know what to do.

I liked Roger. He'd been volunteering one morning a month since the beginning of my legal aid program. He was brilliant. Funny. Extremely good-looking. And ten years younger than me.

I was forty-five years old—and flattered.

★ ★ ★

"How was your day?" Nate asked, coming into the kitchen after work that night. He'd left Beth at the resort for the evening ice-cream social. She was spending the night with Keith.

"Fine." I meant to tell him about my meeting with Roger. But didn't get around to it. I poured us each a glass of wine instead.

"Play for me?" I asked as soon as we'd finished the salad and French bread I'd prepared for dinner.

"I'd rather play *with* you," my handsome husband said, snagging my arm as I walked by him. He slid his hands down my sides, to rest on my hips, pulling my pelvis against his. "We've got the whole night to ourselves."

I did love him. So much. With more vigor than I felt, I pressed my lips to his. And for the next few hours forced myself to focus solely on him.

Two days later Roger asked me to meet him for lunch in his office. He was getting ready to go to trial on a convoluted case and could only spare his lunch hour. He ordered in for us.

"Here's the deal," he said, every inch the professional as he sat behind a big cherrywood desk, with his impeccably knotted tie and crisp white shirt. "Because of the full faith and credit clause, if she and Robert have presented themselves as married for the past seven years in the state of Colorado, she *is* legally married. By common law. We're checking a little further on that.

It depends partially on whether or not an illegal immigrant can have a legal address in this state. The bigger concern is the criminal activity. If she agrees to testify against the brother, she won't be charged as a conspirator. But then there's the issue of criminal neglect of her children. I might not be able to make that go away. It looks like the best I can do, assuming all the other issues work out to her benefit, would be to go for a lesser charge regarding the kids. She'd get probation. And probably have a guardian at litem assigned to them."

He'd been holding my gaze the entire time he was talking.

"Does that mean she'd get to keep them? Under supervision?"

"Most likely."

"But she'd have to testify."

"As far as I can see, it's the only way out. She knowingly stayed, witnessed criminal activity without reporting it. According to what she said the other day, this isn't a one-time thing she can come forward about. It's been going on since they came to the United States."

He was sitting behind his desk, but it still *felt* as though he was touching me, as intimately as he had in the coffeeshop. It certainly was overt, and yet...

"Won't they come after her?" It had to be my imagination. Roger didn't want me. I was merely experiencing the first signs of midlife crisis.

"Not if they're in jail."

"But what if they get off?"

He lifted his hands, let them drop. "We'll ask for protection. There aren't any guarantees."

"What are the chances they'll be convicted?"

"Without all the facts, I couldn't say. But from what I've seen so far, I'd guess pretty good."

Pushing away from his desk, he stood. Moved to a half-size refrigerator across the room and took out a bag.

"I hope you like croissants," he said. "There's a shop around the corner that makes the best chicken salad I've ever had."

He pulled out the sandwiches in their plastic containers and set them on the coffee table in front of the couch before reaching back in for two cans of soda. Popping the tops, he set those down, too, added napkins and patted the seat beside him.

I knew what that meant. Stared at the couch. Caught him watching me. And because I didn't have any idea what else to do, I went and sat there. I might be the owner of a battered women's shelter and co-owner of a ski resort, the mother of three children and a wife of almost twenty-six years, but at that moment I felt like a schoolgirl planning to enter the convent.

I wanted Roger's help. Maria had been sent to me. Through me, Roger would help her.

I wanted to feel young and attractive and desirable. What woman in her forties didn't?

I wanted to be admired by a man who wasn't a generation older than I was.

"You're a very beautiful woman, Eliza."

We'd finished our sandwiches. I was gathering the trash, preparing to throw it away.

"Thank you."

"You have to know I admire you."

Crushing the paper napkins, I half smiled at him. "I admire you, too."

He shifted, perhaps with no hidden agenda. His knee was now touching the outside of my thigh.

"Can I be honest with you?"

I couldn't look at him, but my hands were still clutching the napkins. "Of course."

"I want you, Eliza. I've been thinking about you for months. You keep popping into my head at the oddest moments. While I'm arguing a case in court, driving on the freeway or, here's a good one, out to dinner with another woman."

A little thrill passed through me. I had that much appeal?

"I don't know what to say."

He took my hand. Pried my fingers apart and pulled away the napkins, dropping them on the table. With his fingers he caressed my palms. "Relax."

"I don't think I can do that right now," I whispered.

"Say you'll see me again. Just you and me. No business. Let's go where it takes us."

I gave his suggestion a thought. One. And, extricating my hands, I shook my head and stood.

"I can't tell you how it makes me feel to have someone as successful and good-looking and—" I paused, even smiled "—*young* as you saying these things about me. But, Roger, I am so much in love with my husband I could never, ever think of another man in that way."

Roger, to his credit, bowed out gracefully.

I went straight to the resort. To Nate. And found him coming down the walk with Beth at his side. "We were just going home," he said.

"I have a stomachache." Beth's voice was weak. Whiny. She was pale, too.

"What did you have for lunch?"

"Too much chocolate cake," Nate said, his arm around our daughter as he continued toward his car.

I dug my keys out of my purse. "I'll meet you at the house."

"Can I ride with you?"

My heart seemed to melt as my little girl looked at me with such need. There were times when a mom still got to be a mom.

"Of course. You can lie down when we get home. How about if I read to you? The next chapter in *Jane Eyre.*"

"That would be good, Mommy."

I agreed with my daughter. I'd made a good choice. Several of them that day.

Even if I was the only one who knew it.

★ ★ ★

"You never told me why you showed up at the resort today."

Nate came back to the living room after carrying a sleeping Beth from the couch to her bed. She'd thrown up twice, but then been ravenous an hour later. I let her have a bowl of chicken soup and some crackers while I read to her. If she kept them down all night, she could have whatever she wanted in the morning.

Within reason.

I'd changed from the business suit I'd worn that day into a pair of shorts and a tank top. Nate was still in the shorts and polo shirt he'd worn home from work.

"It was nothing," I said, noticing the lines at his mouth and around his eyes. It had been selfish of me to run to him. To bother him with something I'd already taken care of.

He sat down beside me, giving me the look that made me feel as though I were under a microscope. "*Nothing* wouldn't have brought you all the way out there."

I considered lying to him. Very briefly. Because I didn't want to upset him.

I hadn't acted with Roger in any way that would have dishonored Nate. But if I lied to him, I would be doing so.

"Roger Kempton hit on me today."

Nate stiffened. "Isn't he a little young?"

"He's thirty-four."

"And?"

I turned, peering up at Nate, my heart so full I could hardly speak. "I was flattered," I told him. "But I wasn't the least bit tempted, Nate. I felt *nada*, nothing, zip."

His expression relaxed and he grinned, ran his finger along my lips. "Not even a twinge?"

"Nope. All I could think about was how much I love you. Everyone else will always pale in comparison."

"Oh, woman, what did I ever do to deserve you?" he groaned, pushing me gently down on the couch.

I could have asked him the same question. And would have if my mouth had been free for speaking.

In the fall of 1995, Jimmy called to say he was getting married. I hadn't even realized he'd had a girlfriend after Anita, who hadn't worked out.

"How long have you known this girl?" was the first question I asked, motioning Nate to pick up the other phone so he could listen in.

"Forever," my son said. "You know her, too. Remember Lindsay?"

I did. And two months later, when my twenty-five-year-old middle child stood at the front of the church with his bride in a Christmas wedding, I sat in the front row holding back tears as I remembered back to his fifteenth year. He'd come into the kitchen one night while I was finishing some gourmet meal I'd prepared during Elizabeth's naptime that day. It'd been during one of the darkest times of my life—the year without Nate. And my son, whose voice was still cracking and who hadn't yet started to shave, told me in all seriousness that he'd met the girl he was going to marry.

Funny how life worked sometimes. After all the years, all the women, it turned out he was right.

The following spring, Keith showed up at Beth's thirteenth birthday dinner with a pretty blonde in tow.

"Everyone, this is Emily," he said.

"Oh! Hi!" Beth greeted her with a grin, pulling out the chair next to her. "Sit here."

Emily sat. Keith took the adjacent chair. And that was that.

Until after dinner.

"We have something to tell you," Keith said after Beth had opened her last present. "Emily graduated from UC this month and we're going to get married."

My jaw dropped. I might have embarrassed myself totally, made some less than congratulatory remark, like *it would've been nice to meet her at any point in the last three years,* had Nate not been sitting next to me. He put his hand on my thigh under the table, and probably to make sure he was getting enough of my attention to distract me, slid his fingers higher, too.

I asked if I could do anything to help with the wedding.

"Well, that's just it, Mom," Keith said. "Emily and I were hoping you'd help her with everything. Her mom took off when she was a kid and it's just her and her dad, and he's not real good with stuff like this."

I glanced at Emily, saw the apprehensive but hopeful look on her face, fell in love, and forgave them everything.

The wedding wasn't big, but it was beautiful. We held it at the resort in August of that year, with Emily's father officiating. Jimmy and Lindsay were a joy to watch, obviously so besotted with each other.

Lori and Charles couldn't make it. They'd already booked their vacations that year—a six-week world cruise. It had been several years since we'd seen them, but we still talked on the phone at least once a month.

Alice, June and Bonnie came out with their husbands, no kids. William and Shelly did, too. It was great to have so much of my family together again.

Beth, one of the attendants, was beautiful in her long pink gown that hugged a figure that was starting to look a bit too womanly for my liking.

Or Nate's. He watched our daughter like a hawk all night, interrupting anytime a young man got close enough to ask her to dance.

"Lighten up, daddy," I said to him about halfway through the evening when he'd taken a break from the piano to once again waylay our daughter. "She's growing up."

"Over my dead body." Nate's voice was gruff as he said the words. And then he chuckled. "She's not going to be easy, is she?"

"Nope." I ran my finger along the nape of his neck. "But not much that matters ever is."

Chapter 18

Nate turned sixty-two in 1997, twenty-nine years after I married him. I threw a party for him at the resort. With enough notice, Lori and Charles were able to make it. All of my family, sans nieces and nephews, were there, as well. Alice had turned sixty that year, and was complaining of osteoporosis. I hated to see my siblings aging.

But if I had a moment or two of terror as I considered the years to come, I hid them well. And concentrated on all the love surrounding me as we celebrated. The shelter was doing well. Maria was now working there as a house-mother; she was a legal citizen due to her common-law marriage and on probation, maintaining custody of her children, while her husband and his brother spent the next twenty-five years in prison. The shelter had received enough funding for another year. The resort was expanding again. Keith and Emily were expecting their first child. And at fourteen, Beth was taller than I was.

That same year, a one-hundred-and-fifteen-year-old man, John Bell, received a new pacemaker. And actor Tony Randall, at age seventy-seven, fathered his first child. I made sure Nate was apprised of both facts. My husband often mentioned retiring, but never did anything about it. And he took to the slopes that winter, just like always.

Princess Diana died that year. And Timothy McVeigh was sentenced to death for the Oklahoma City bombings. In today's world, no one was safe. Not princesses and not small children playing in day cares. I wondered what the sisters at St. Catherine made of it all. How they found peace.

And then, two days before Christmas, I got a call from my oldest son. He and Emily were at the hospital. They'd just given birth to a 7 pound 6 ounce boy. And I understood all over again that to combat all the evil in the world, there were miracles, and to overcome hate, there was love.

They were naming the baby Nathaniel Keith.

I didn't say anything, but I thought they were giving that guy impossible odds with two such huge pairs of shoes to fill.

Calling out to Nate with the phone still in my hand, I grabbed my coat and purse, and paced impatiently while he started the car and brought it around to the front of the house, where the walk had been shoveled. We made it to the hospital in record time.

And at forty-eight, I was a grandma.

Jimmy and Lindsay had a little girl the following year. They called her Kyle Elizabeth, and Beth promptly changed her name back to the one on her birth certificate.

I didn't spend quite as much time at the shelter as I once had, but only because I was busy being a grandma. I babysat any chance I got, and was thrilled to find I hadn't lost my touch. I could still change a diaper and simultaneously wipe a nose.

Nate was as eager as I was to spend time with the grandkids. He even paid for a three-day cruise for both of our sons and their wives at Christmas so we'd have the babies to ourselves.

Where I seemed to have lost my touch was with teenagers. My fifteen-year-old daughter was giving me a hellish time. She had two interests, soccer and boys, and had determined that I knew nothing about either. If I said something was black, she insisted it was white. And if I was proven correct, she'd either sulk for days or go into a fit of hysterics.

With her father, however, she was an angel.

They said every cloud had a silver lining.

Once again, Nate was mine.

Elizabeth wanted a car for her sixteenth birthday. We gave her a ticket to fly to London and spend a week with

Lori and Charles. And told her she wouldn't be getting her driver's license for at least a year. She started to argue—until Jimmy, with baby Kyle on his lap, piped up that he'd had to wait, too. That took the wind out her sails. She called all her friends and bragged about going to Europe.

That fall and early winter, late in '99, Nate went skiing with all three of his kids. I still skied a bit, but I'd never been the athlete they all were. Elizabeth kept up with her brothers, daring to take slopes I didn't even want to know about.

And maybe that was why I found it odd that she turned down a trip with her brothers and their wives to Tahoe the first weekend in December. She said she had to study for finals. Which she did. But schoolwork generally came easily to Elizabeth—to all three of my kids— and Nate and I were going to look after the babies, which wouldn't leave the house all that conducive to study. Still, she was in her sophomore year of high school, the critical year for gaining college scholarships, and the babies would have naps.

On Saturday morning of that weekend, she was up by nine—at least two hours before she normally rolled out of bed.

"Hi." With her long hair up in a series of fashionable clips, and wearing sweat pants, a long-sleeved shirt that left a strip of her belly bare and oversize Disney-character bedroom slippers, she slid into a chair in the kitchen. I was just finishing the last of the breakfast dishes. I'd made bacon and eggs for Nate.

He was in the living room, on the floor with our grandbabies and an assortment of expensive learning toys.

"You're up early." I smiled at her over my shoulder. "Would you like some breakfast? There's eggs left. Or I can make some oatmeal."

"Oatmeal would be nice." She laid her head on the table. "And some toast?"

Glad to have my daughter in the room with me, I happily complied. Feeding my children satisfied me. It always had. And while I moved about the kitchen, Elizabeth chatted. About school. A boy she thought was cute. Another who was a jerk.

All talk that was good for my soul. She was letting me in.

"Thanks, Mom," she said when I set her breakfast before her, complete with jam, napkin, spoon and glass of juice.

"You're welcome." I wanted to sit with her, but was afraid to cramp her style so she'd back off. Instead, I spent a long time rinsing out one pan, wiping a few crumbs, putting a knife in the dishwasher.

She asked what her father and I were doing that day. Talked about the order in which she'd chosen to study her subjects, giving me a verbal outline that encompassed both Saturday and Sunday. She wondered if I thought her plan would work.

I assured her it was fine.

"And hey, as a reward for spending my weekend on the grind, would it be okay if I slept at JoAnn's?"

"Tonight?"

"I'll be home by noon tomorrow, I promise."

Elizabeth didn't get up for church anymore. And I wasn't going the next day due to the babies. Still, I hesitated.

"Doesn't she have to study?"

"She's at it all day, too."

"Let me guess, you both got up early."

"Yep. We synched our alarm clocks last night."

It all sounded so normal. So teenage. Yet something didn't feel right to me.

Elizabeth was busy eating. She hadn't looked up once since she'd mentioned JoAnn. Not only that, she usually asked if she could spend the night with a girlfriend. Not sleep at her house.

Teen vernacular changed daily. I understood that. But...

"I don't think so, honey," I said. "Not tonight. It doesn't seem fair to your brothers that you turned them down and then go off to spend the night with your girlfriend."

"Come on, Mom! It's one night instead of a whole weekend."

I could see the logic in that. "And since it's only one night, it's not going to kill you to stay home. I'm really proud of you for putting your studies first this weekend. If you go to JoAnn's and the two of you gab half the night, then you aren't going to be fresh for tomorrow's day with the books."

She swore at me. Something that had started the summer before. I didn't validate it with a response.

"I'm going to ask Dad," she said, but ate every morsel of the food I'd prepared before she went in to do so.

I wasn't worried about Nate. He backed me up every single time. Elizabeth knew that, too. I think she just said things like that to get at me. So I tried not to let it happen.

Clearing the table, I finished in the kitchen, preparing myself for the treatment I'd likely get from my daughter that day. It might be what I'd termed the snipes. Biting my head off whenever I made a comment or even walked into a room. Or maybe she'd play the injured-baby role, designed, I figured, to gain my sympathy. It sometimes worked. The worst, to me, was the cold war. She'd treat me as though I weren't there, refusing to answer if I spoke to her.

Well, she'd get over it. She always did. And I'd have Nate and the babies with me all day.

It was the cold war in the morning. Moving to the snipes over lunch. And the pathetic baby by dinnertime. I couldn't remember a day I'd gotten all three. Oddest of all, by the time Elizabeth went to bed, tired from studying, she gave me a hug good-night.

I got hugs most nights. Had from the boys, too, even when they were teenagers. But never from Elizabeth on her angry days.

Her way of punishing me, I suppose.

But she'd hugged me good-night. Could it be that she was growing up?

Usually Nate and I went to bed late on Saturdays. The habit had probably started when the boys were teenagers. We had a rule about not going to sleep until all our children were safely at home. But that night, with everyone accounted for, we went up just after eleven.

Nate's step was a little slow as he climbed, and I knew that chasing around after two toddlers had exhausted him. Heck, I was aching myself.

Elizabeth's door was closed—which was something she'd begun doing the year before.

That had never deterred me. Quietly, not wanting to wake my testy child and incur more wrath, I opened the door, just as I did every night, needing to see her peaceful before I could fall asleep. Some nights I had to stay up reading far longer than I wanted to, waiting for her to turn off her light and fall asleep before I could peek in.

And any night I hadn't done so, Nate had.

"I'll look in on the little ones," he said now. "You need to go to her tonight."

He knew me so well. After the day I'd had with the daughter I adored, I did need a moment with her when my heart could be completely open, unprotected. When I could just stand there a moment in the darkness and love her.

Turning the knob, as I had thousands of times before,

I slowly pushed open the door. The very first thing I noticed was a small piece of her curtain caught in the window. It hadn't been that way earlier.

She'd had her window open? In December?

Had she been smoking in her room? No—I would've noticed the smell on her skin, her hair.

Fully inside now, I approached the bed, defending my heart against the wounds Elizabeth inflicted at random. It hurt, anyway when I saw the shape beneath her covers and the hair on her pillow. The shape was a couple of pillows. And the hair? I pulled. Out from the covers came a doll I'd given her when she was seven because it had hair exactly like hers.

"Nate!" My voice was soft enough not to wake the babies, but urgent just the same.

"What?" His earlier lethargy was completely gone as he appeared beside me.

"Look at this."

He glanced from the bed, to the window and back. "I'll be damned."

I called JoAnn's mom. There was no answer. I can't say I was surprised.

"I'm guessing that young lady's family is gone for the weekend," I told Nate, hanging up the phone in our bedroom.

He'd changed into sweats when we'd settled in to watch a movie that evening, but was now pulling on a pair of jeans. I kept mine on, too.

"The girls might be there, but if they saw our number on caller ID, they're not answering," I said.

"I had the same thought." Nate grabbed his wallet, shoved it into his pocket. "I'm going there first."

I nodded, running downstairs behind him. We weren't the type to sit at home and wait, but one of us had to stay with the babies. And Nate was much safer out alone at night than I was.

"Drive carefully." He was at the back door, holding his keys, and turned to look at me.

His features softening, he hooked a hand around my neck, drawing me against his chest. "Don't worry, Liza. We'll find her."

I tried so hard not to cry. "I just hope she's okay," I said as the tears came anyway. "She was so angry with me. You don't think she ran away, do you?"

Elizabeth had left the ladder she'd used to escape propped up against the side of the house.

With his forehead on mine Nate asked, "Do you?"

I couldn't get beyond the fear and the panic. "I don't know."

"Why'd you tell her she couldn't spend the night with JoAnn?"

"I don't know. I just had this feeling…"

"And when have your feelings ever led you wrong?"

Never. Not once. That knowledge had grown solid over the years.

"What this tells me is that the two of them had something planned. Wherever she is tonight, it isn't because she's lashing out at you. It's where she planned to be all along."

"Alone with JoAnn because her parents are gone?"

"Or at a party," he said, his voice grim.

"Call me when you get to JoAnn's," I told him, thankful now that he'd insisted on getting us car phones. "In the meantime, I'm calling some of her other friends, to find out if there was anything going on tonight."

She was going to hate us for this. I didn't think her friends' parents, would, however. They all had teenage daughters, too.

The only thing we accomplished that night, besides wasting a lot of gas, was to alert three of Elizabeth's friends' parents that their daughters were not where they were supposed to be. Two of the girls had told their parents they were staying at each other's houses. Another, like Elizabeth, had climbed out her window.

We all determined that there were boys involved in the night's escapade, but none of us had last names or phone numbers. Elizabeth had yet to go out on a real date where I'd be privy to that information. And we all agreed to call everyone else as soon as we heard from any of our daughters.

That left the rest of the hours until dawn—or until Elizabeth reappeared—to sit and wait. Nate and I talked for a while. About the shelter. The state's regulations only allowed women to stay in government shelters for a limited period of time. Often it wasn't long enough to let them reshape their lives and make a clean start. I didn't have that rule and currently had two families who'd been there for more than two years. One of them was Maria's. In my work at the Boulder women's shelter, I knew I'd come full circle from my life at St. Catherine's as I spent my days serving those who were less fortunate than I was.

And Nate talked about the resort. About how well Keith was doing. He was considering exchanging his CEO position with Keith's vice-presidential spot. My heart tripped a bit as he voiced the thought. I hated to see this sign that life was moving on yet again. But I'd known it was coming.

Needed to come.

We tried to watch television. To talk about the babies and their futures. And all the while my heart grew heavier, my stomach more knotted. It was four o'clock in the morning. No good happened to sixteen-year-old girls out at that hour of the night.

My mind played all sorts of scenarios for me. From dead on the side of the road, to deep in the woods someplace, the victim of a fiend who was doing God knows what.

Please, God. Oh, please, keep her safe. Whatever she's done, please forgive her. Surround her with your angels. Protect her and bring her home to me.

"Where is she?" I finally cried out, jumping from the end of the couch where I'd spent much of the night.

"I can tell you where she's going to wish she was," Nate said, joining me at the window.

He sounded fierce, but I knew he was just as worried.

"None of the others have called," I said. "So at least we can assume they're still together."

And hope there was safety in numbers.

At six o'clock, the phone rang. I fumbled it on the way to my ear.

"Hello?"

"Mom?" Elizabeth was crying.

"Elizabeth? Where are you? What's wrong?"

All I could think of was my baby girl raped. Bloody. In a hospital. But alive.

Thank God, she was alive.

"We're in Longmont." About fifteen miles away. "We went to an all-night concert in Fort Collins and it started to snow on the way home and the oil light in JoAnn's mom's car came on and we thought we could make it, but then the car started to smoke and then it just died."

My heart was pounding so hard I could barely hear.

"Are you all right?"

"Yes, we're fine. But… Nothing went like it was supposed to."

"Where in Longmont are you?" I dealt with the first priority.

She didn't know. On the side of the highway just past the Longmont exit. She was using JoAnn's mom's car phone.

Nate, listening in, told her to stay put. He was on his way and would call her from his car.

Again, I sat and waited.

★ ★ ★

Nate had pretty much let her have it by the time they pulled into the driveway just before eight o'clock on Sunday morning. Kyle and Nathaniel, changed and dressed already, sat in their high chairs munching on Cheerios as Nate and Elizabeth came through the door.

"Mom!" Elizabeth ran to me, clutching me tightly. And while I hugged her back, more thankful than she could probably imagine to have her home, I also maintained some distance.

What Elizabeth had done this time was far more serious than mean words or pouting.

"I made a breakfast casserole," I said, pulling the sausage, egg and cheese concoction from the oven. "Sit down and eat and then, after you've rested, we'll talk."

A very docile sixteen-year-old quietly sat down at the table. She only picked at her breakfast but sat there until I excused her to go have a shower and a nap.

She and her father didn't exchange a single word the entire time.

Thankfully, the babies, unaware of the underlying tension, babbled on.

Chapter 19

"What's the one thing you told me you absolutely could not tolerate, no matter how much you loved me?" Elizabeth and I were at the kitchen table early that afternoon, while Nate tried to get the babies down for a nap.

"Lying to me," I answered my recalcitrant daughter. My heart was heavy with grief and disappointment. Despite my gratitude for her safety, I couldn't relent, couldn't let her off that easily. All day long, the things that could've happened to those girls last night—even before they'd broken down—had run through my mind.

"And I didn't," Elizabeth said. "Heck, Mom, lying to you would be like lying to God."

My heart jolted. I wanted so badly to hug her and beg her to promise me she'd never, ever do anything like this again.

"You deliberately deceived me."

"I would've slept at JoAnn's if you said I could. I just wouldn't have got there until early this morning."

I'd *known* that the way she'd asked had signified something remiss. Too bad I'd underestimated her determination and the lengths she'd go to get what she wanted.

"I didn't say you out-and-out told a lie, I said you deliberately deceived me, which is essentially the same thing. You knew I'd think you were at JoAnn's all night, which you never intended to be. Furthermore—" I was on a roll now as all the panic, the worry and the pain of the past twenty-four hours, perhaps the past few years, came rushing back. "Last night, you hugged me goodnight, wanting me to believe you were going upstairs to your room for the rest of the night. You never intended to do that, either."

"I know."

Her acquiescence took me off guard. I pinned her with a stare meant to make her squirm.

"Believe me, Mom, I know everything you want to say to me. I have your voice in my head everywhere I go."

She had my voice in her head. That was the nicest thing the kid had ever said to me in her life. And she didn't even know it. Which made it that much nicer.

"You don't need to say any of it," she muttered next.

"Because your father's already said it all?" I asked.

"No, because I'd already figured it out for myself before we left town. At first, climbing out the window was kind of fun. An adventure. And I was mad 'cause the reason you wouldn't let me stay at JoAnn's was so lame." She stopped then, looked at me curiously. "Why wouldn't you?"

I shrugged. "I don't know. I just had a feeling."

Sighing, Elizabeth continued. "After I got out of the house and JoAnn started to pull away, I felt gross. All I could think of was you and Daddy back there, trusting me. And the babies and how cute they are. And, I don't know...I just wanted to be home."

"Then why didn't you come back?"

"What was I going to tell JoAnn? I'd look like a chicken. Or a little mama's girl."

"Or a very smart young woman."

"Believe me, I know." She sighed again. "I can't tell you how many times last night I would rather have looked like the biggest chicken ever. I kept trying to have fun with the rest of them, but I just couldn't."

The pressure in my chest was dissipating rapidly.

"You're going to be grounded. You know that, right?"

She nodded. "Dad told me."

"And you've lost any trust I had in letting you go places with JoAnn."

Bowing her head, she said, "I'm not sure I'm going to hang out with her much, anyway," she said.

I raised my head sharply. "Did she do things last night that she shouldn't have?"

"Like drugs and drinking, you mean?"

"Yes."

"Yeah, she did."

"Did you?"

"No." She was still looking me straight in the eye.

"Good. I'm glad to hear it." So glad, that if she weren't sitting there needing me to be stiff and stern, I'd have hauled her into my arms for the longest hug of our lives.

"Can I ask you something?" Her gaze was curious. And sweet.

"Yes."

"How'd you know to look in my room last night?"

Covering her hand with mine, I told her, "I've looked in your room every night since the day you were born. And I'll continue to do so every night that we spend under the same roof."

"Because of Sarah?"

"Nope. Because of you."

During her last two years of high school, Elizabeth was a model child. Not once after the night of the concert in Fort Collins did she give us any cause for doubt. She dated some, but always brought the boy to meet us first, left us with numbers and was home by curfew. She made straight As and earned herself a scholarship to her brothers' alma mater.

Nate had switched titles with Keith at the resort and worked shorter hours. He played the piano a lot in those days—the same disfigured piano we'd had all those years—and while I hated to leave him alone, I was only fifty-one and needed more stimulation than I could get sitting at home. The shelter was as busy as ever. We'd had an offer from the city to erect a sister project on the other side of town. I wouldn't own that one, but I'd agreed to be a consultant as long as they needed me.

And then, the year I turned fifty-two, my baby girl left home to go to college. I'd thought I was fully prepared, but as August drew near and we were buying everything she'd need for her dorm room, I'd have moments when I couldn't move. When I just wanted to lie on the couch and let life pass me by.

We'd made it through Y-2000 intact, and here I was, in the fall of 2001, falling apart.

Nate found me one day during the first week in September, flat on my back in the living room with no television on, no book to read and no real desire to rest.

"I was thinking about taking a cruise around the world," he said, lifting my feet and holding them on his lap as he sat down. "Want to come with me?"

"Could we stop off in London?"

The thought of that brought back a bit of the anticipation, the excitement, I'd had trouble finding.

"Lori's expecting us the first of October."

That got me up in a hurry. "You already have the trip booked?"

He pulled an envelope out of his back pocket and handed it to me. "I spoke to Maria. She's got things covered at the shelter and she'll e-mail Lori if there's anything urgent that needs your attention."

I couldn't believe this. Mouth open, I stared at him, and then at the envelope. "How long are we going to be gone?"

"Six weeks."

"We'll be home in time for Thanksgiving?"

"Of course."

"Really?"

Nate stood beside me, leaning in to touch his lips to mine. "Really."

"When do we leave?"

"Next week." He turned to go. "Which gives you five days to buy yourself some new negligees," he said. "I'm finally going to get my honeymoon."

We didn't make the cruise that year. On September 11th, 2001, our country was attacked by terrorists, killing more than 3000 innocent people. Elizabeth came home. Keith and Jimmy and their families came home. There was nothing any of us could do except watch the television and pray.

But we were together.

We had to be.

Nate and I took our cruise the following spring. Traveling was harder now, but the honeymoon part was worth it.

The years seemed to go by like months after that. The winter Olympics were in Salt Lake in 2002 and Nate treated us all to an unforgettable week. We'd never traveled as a family, stayed in a hotel together, since the boys got married, and while we had to adjust to different routines, there wasn't one problem the entire trip.

Nate and I traveled to California for an extended stay the next fall. My brother and sisters were all getting older, were all grandparents, and our time with them was dear to me. Alice introduced me to the pleasures of slot machines and as soon as I got home, I sought out the closest casino so I'd know where to get a fix if I needed one. So far, the most I'd won was six hundred dollars. The most I'd lost, half of that.

I never had been a big spender.

A new George Bush was president and in May of that year, he announced the end of combat in a new war, America's war against Iraq, begun shortly after 9/11.

It didn't end though.

On April 2, 2005, Pope John Paul II died. More than four million people traveled to the Vatican to mourn him. I wasn't one of them. I'd been away from the Church for more years than I'd been a part of it.

Yet, alone in the privacy of my bedroom, I wept.

It was my month for crying. Elizabeth graduated a few weeks after the Pope's death and as I watched my baby walk across that stage with such purpose, take her diploma and wave at her father and me, I knew in my heart that an era had just ended.

I didn't know about the surprise she had waiting for us after the ceremony.

"Mom, Dad, this is Ronald," she said to us, pulling a bespectacled, skinny man to her side. I didn't like the way she hugged his arm so familiarly to her breast.

"Mrs. Grady, Mr. Grady," the young man said, shaking our hands with a firm grip. "It's good to finally meet you."

I did like his direct gaze.

"Ronald has one year left of a five-year premed program," she said.

I found out later that night,.over dinner, that he was also living with my daughter. And that they planned to continue the arrangement until he graduated from school, at which time they would marry.

I smiled. Welcomed him to the family. And sobbed all the way back to Boulder, where Nate silently took me in his arms and held on tight.

Two thousand six is not a year I remember well. In April, shortly after what turned out to be the last snowfall of the year, Nate went out for a hike to see how winter had left the trails we used for our summer camps. It was a hike he'd taken every year since we'd purchased the resort. He'd bring a saw and some water and head out, moving trees that had fallen across the paths, or sawing a walk through them. He'd make note of danger zones due to mudslides, embed stones where they were needed to make safer stepping places.

The day had always been kind of sacred with him. An ending and a beginning.

In 2006, Nate didn't come back. Dinnertime came

and went. I called Keith at the resort and he assumed his father had missed him after the hike, that he'd gone home.

Jimmy met us at the house. Elizabeth and Ronald drove down from Fort Collins, and together with my children, I waited for word from the rescue teams that had been dispatched.

He was found the next morning, just as the sun was rising, wandering around the edge of a field on the other side of the mountain. It was a small mountain, close to the resort. One he'd climbed many times.

But this particular time he hadn't been able to find his way back.

Many trips to the doctor later, it was discovered that Nate had a rare condition called Pick's Disease—a relatively benign-sounding name that meant the frontal lobe of his brain was deteriorating. The long-term diagnosis was a dementia so debilitating he wouldn't even be able to get himself to the bathroom. He was only seventy-one years old.

I found him sitting at the piano the night we found out. Just sitting.

"Play something for me," I said, sliding down beside him, my hip pressing his.

"I'm scared, Liza."

Covering his hand where it lay on his lap, I held on tight. "I know. Me, too."

"I can't bear the thought of you having to spend your days changing my pants."

That sent panic racing through me. And a peculiar calm, as well. "I'll be honored to do it. You and I are one, Nate. Taking care of you is just taking care of me and as long as I have you—in any version—I'm blessed."

"I won't allow it." He'd been vacillating between anger and a frightening, helpless giving up all day.

"I remember once a very smart man explaining to me that there are things we can't control in life, but that we still have to live. As I recall, he hauled me out of bed and forced me to clean strangers' bathrooms."

"This is different."

"Every single challenge we've ever met in this life has been different from all the others. But one thing remains the same and it's the one thing that sees us through every time."

His eyes were moist with unshed tears as he turned to face me, the lines around his mouth, his eyes, more pronounced than I'd ever seen them. That night, for the first time, he looked old to me.

"Our love," he finally said.

I nodded, and swallowed the lump in my throat. "Please play for me."

He started slowly, as though exploring the keys for the first time, running his fingers along the cracked edges, picking out a note, then two. Tears fell from my eyes as I watched him, knowing he was thinking about a time when he'd no longer remember how to make music.

I couldn't think about what was to come. Doing that would prevent me from getting through the next days and months.

Nate played for hours that night and I sat right beside him on that hard bench, wondering if he knew that he'd played "My Cup Runneth Over" four times.

I spent every moment with Nate after that. He could live to be a hundred—his doctor said he still had the body of a much younger man—but I had no idea how long he'd be with me in the ways that mattered. The kids came home every weekend and we'd have big dinners and singalongs at the piano.

And at night, after making love to me—sometimes desperately—Nate would talk about the future. And the past. About life. We'd cry some. Mostly I held him and told him I'd store everything in my mind for both of us. Even when he was no longer conscious of them, his memories would always be safe with me.

In early 2007 Nate got a bladder infection. He was hospitalized due to a high fever, and two days later his doctor told me that Nate's body was shutting down. One by one, his organs were stopping. They said the infection had spread.

They gave him a day, two at the most.

I'd never heard of anyone dying of a bladder infection.

Stunned, existing in a cocoon of disbelief, I called my children. And then I sat.

At fifty-eight, I was not ready to face a future without him.

★ ★ ★

I'm sitting beside Nate's bed now, holding his hand. He's sleeping peacefully, or perhaps he's slipped into the coma that will eventually take him. He hasn't opened his eyes in more than twenty-four hours. I haven't let go of his hand, either, except to go to the bathroom once in a while. When my eyes get too weary, I lean forward and lay my head on his stomach; while I drift into sleep, I can feel the steady rise and fall of his breathing.

The kids are all here. They've been in this room with me, night and day, for the past six days. They hold me together, offer a comfort I can't describe, and yet they can't reach me in the world I'm inhabiting. Only Nate and I are there. Only Nate and I have ever been there.

I feel his hand squeeze mine—his first voluntary motion in more than a day—and my heart jumps. I've known all along that he'll show them. He'll beat the odds. He always does.

He's been here six days instead of the two they gave him.

He isn't going to leave me this soon. It isn't time yet.

I glance up. He's staring straight at me and he's got that look in his eyes. The one that tells me he sees only me, that I am everything beautiful in the world to him.

He looks like he's trying to speak. His chin moves. The tip of his tongue comes out, as though he's trying to lick his lips. In spite of all the ice chips I've been rubbing over them, the chap stick, they are so dry.

Some part of me recognizes that the kids are roused

by his movement. They're standing at the end of the bed, but they can't penetrate our space.

Finally, after obvious struggle, he manages to mouth one word. I read it clearly. *Love.*

And my heart speaks to me. There can be no anger now. No fight. I have to love him enough to let him do what he needs to do. I have to let go.

Standing up, never breaking eye contact with my husband, I nod. And try not to cry. I climb into the bed with him, kiss those lips, moistening them gently with my tongue, and I hold him while he passes away to the next phase of his life without me.

I don't recognize the animal cry that tears through and out of me. There are no words, nothing even human. I know it's the sound of my heart and soul erupting from the body I've been given to see me through this life—separating from it.

Hands touch my shoulders, arms come around me, but they can't reach me.

I am devastated. Empty. And scared.

I think I'm alone. I'm not sure. My children might be in the room, but they've backed away from the bed. They understand how it is with Nate and me. They *know.*

I don't have any sense of how long I've been lying here. Gradually I become aware that I'm going to have to move. And as I think about doing that, it's as though Nate's there behind me, lifting me up, whispering to me.

And I'm reminded of the day after Elizabeth's all-night concert, her sweet words telling me that my voice is always in her head. Just as Nate's will always be in mine.

He's telling me I'm a blessed woman. I've lived life fully, with all my heart, guided by my heart, and that guidance will be there for the rest of my days on this earth.

He tells me I knew it all. That in the things that matter, I will always know.

And when I pass on, Nate and I will continue walking side by side.

We are not apart, dear reader, we are only separated for a time. Our hearts recognized each other instantly the night we met, and nothing in our imperfect human existence could change that.

With Nate's strength, and my own, I climb out of bed. I have chores to do. Grandchildren to teach. Memories to keep alive. And a love to cherish.

* * * * *

Set in darkness beyond the ordinary world.
Passionate tales of life and death.
With characters' lives ruled by laws the everyday
world can't begin to imagine.

n●cturne

It's time to discover the Raintree trilogy…

New York Times *bestselling author*
LINDA HOWARD
brings you the dramatic first book
RAINTREE: INFERNO

The Ansara Wizards are rising and the Raintree clan
must rejoin the battle against their foes, testing their
powers, relationships and forcing upon them lives they
never could have imagined before…

Turn the page for a sneak preview
of the captivating first book
in the Raintree trilogy,
RAINTREE: INFERNO
by LINDA HOWARD
On sale April 2

Dante Raintree stood with his arms crossed as he watched the woman on the monitor. The image was in black and white to better show details; color distracted the brain. He focused on her hands, watching every move she made, but what struck him most was how uncommonly *still* she was. She didn't fidget or play with her chips, or look around at the other players. She peeked once at her down card, then didn't touch it again, signaling for another hit by tapping a fingernail on the table. Just because she didn't seem to be paying attention to the other players, though, didn't mean she was as unaware as she seemed.

"What's her name?" Dante asked.

"Lorna Clay," replied his chief of security, Al Rayburn.

"At first I thought she was counting, but she doesn't pay enough attention."

"She's paying attention, all right," Dante murmured. "You just don't see her doing it." A card counter had to remember every card played. Supposedly counting cards was impossible with the number of decks used by the casinos, but there were those rare individuals who could calculate the odds even with multiple decks.

"I thought that, too," said Al. "But look at this piece of tape coming up. Someone she knows comes up to her and speaks, she looks around and starts chatting, completely misses the play of the people to her left—and doesn't look around even when the deal comes back to her, just taps that finger. And damn if she didn't win. Again."

Dante watched the tape, rewound it, watched it again. Then he watched it a third time. There had to be something he was missing, because he couldn't pick out a single giveaway.

"If she's cheating," Al said with something like respect, "she's the best I've ever seen."

"What does your gut say?"

Al scratched the side of his jaw, considering. Finally, he said, "If she isn't cheating, she's the luckiest person walking. She wins. Week in, week out, she wins. Never a huge amount, but I ran the numbers and she's into us for about five grand a week. Hell, boss, on her way out of the casino she'll stop by a slot machine, feed a dollar in and walk away with at least fifty. It's never the same machine, either. I've had her watched, I've had her followed, I've even looked for the same faces in the casino every time she's in here, and I can't find a common denominator."

"Is she here now?"

"She came in about half an hour ago. She's playing blackjack, as usual."

"Bring her to my office," Dante said, making a swift decision. "Don't make a scene."

"Got it," said Al, turning on his heel and leaving the security center.

Dante left, too, going up to his office. His face was calm. Normally he would leave it to Al to deal with a cheater, but he was curious. How was she doing it? There were a lot of bad cheaters, a few good ones, and every so often one would come along who was the stuff of which legends were made: the cheater who didn't get caught, even when people were alert and the camera was on him—or, in this case, her.

It was possible to simply be lucky, as most people understood luck. Chance could turn a habitual loser into a big-time winner. Casinos, in fact, thrived on that hope. But luck itself wasn't habitual, and he knew that what passed for luck was often something else: cheating. And there was the other kind of luck, the kind he himself possessed, but it depended not on chance but on who and what he was. He knew it was an innate power and not Dame Fortune's erratic smile. Since power like his was rare, the odds made it likely the woman he'd been watching was merely a very clever cheat.

Her skill could provide her with a very good living, he thought, doing some swift calculations in his head. Five grand a week equaled $260,000 a year, and that was just from his casino. She probably hit them all, careful to keep the numbers relatively low so she stayed under the radar.

He wondered how long she'd been taking him, how long she'd been winning a little here, a little there, before Al noticed.

The curtains were open on the wall-to-wall window in his office, giving the impression, when one first opened the door, of stepping out onto a covered balcony. The glazed window faced west, so he could catch the sunsets. The sun was low now, the sky painted in purple and gold. At his home in the mountains, most of the windows faced east, affording him views of the sunrise. Something in him needed both the greeting and the goodbye of the sun. He'd always been drawn to sunlight, maybe because fire was his element to call, to control.

He checked his internal time: four minutes until sundown. Without checking the sunrise tables every day, he knew exactly when the sun would slide behind the mountains. He didn't own an alarm clock. He didn't need one. He was so acutely attuned to the sun's position that he had only to check within himself to know the time. As for waking at a particular time, he was one of those people who could tell himself to wake at a certain time, and he did. That talent had nothing to do with being Raintree, so he didn't have to hide it; a lot of perfectly ordinary people had the same ability.

He had other talents and abilities, however, that did require careful shielding. The long days of summer instilled in him an almost sexual high, when he could feel contained power buzzing just beneath his skin. He had to be doubly careful not to cause candles to leap into flame just by his presence, or to start wildfires with a glance in the dry-as-tinder brush. He loved Reno; he didn't want to burn it down. He just felt so damn *alive* with all the sunshine pouring down that he wanted to let the energy pour through him instead of holding it inside.

This must be how his brother Gideon felt while pulling lightning, all that hot power searing through his muscles, his veins. They had this in common, the connection with raw power. All the members of the far-flung Raintree clan had some power, some heightened ability, but only members of the royal family could channel and control the earth's natural energies.

Dante wasn't just of the royal family, he was the Dranir, the leader of the entire clan. "Dranir" was synonymous with king, but the position he held wasn't ceremonial, it was one of sheer power. He was the oldest son of the previous Dranir, but he would have been passed over for the position if he hadn't also inherited the power to hold it.

Behind him came Al's distinctive knock on the door. The outer office was empty, Dante's secretary having gone home hours before. "Come in," he called, not turning from his view of the sunset.

The door opened, and Al said, "Mr. Raintree, this is Lorna Clay."

Dante turned and looked at the woman, all his senses on alert. The first thing he noticed was the vibrant color of her hair, a rich, dark red that encompassed a multitude of shades from copper to burgundy. The warm amber light danced along the iridescent strands, and he felt a hard tug of sheer lust in his gut. Looking at her hair was almost like looking at fire, and he had the same reaction.

The second thing he noticed was that she was spitting mad.

EVERLASTING LOVE™
Every great love has a story to tell™

"Joelle and Bobby…I'm aware my visit might have been difficult for you."

Difficult? In fact, nothing will ever be the same again for Joelle Webber and Bobby DiFranco. They've built careers and a home, raised a family. They've shaped a life of trust, understanding and support. It all would have remained rock-solid if not for the unexpected intrusion of Joelle's ex and the long-buried secret he unearths. Joelle and Bobby have leaned on each other through countless crises, but this time the very foundation of their marriage is shaken.

Can they put it back together one more time?

Look for
The Marriage Bed
by
Judith Arnold
available this May.

www.eHarlequin.com

HETMB0507

REQUEST YOUR FREE BOOKS!

2 FREE NOVELS PLUS 2 FREE GIFTS!

 HARLEQUIN®

EVERLASTING LOVE™

Every great love has a story to tell™

YES! Please send me 2 FREE Harlequin® Everlasting Love™ novels and my 2 FREE gifts. After receiving them, if I don't wish to receive any more books, I can return the shipping statement marked "cancel." If I don't cancel, I will receive 4 brand-new novels every other month and be billed just $4.47 per book in the U.S. or $4.99 per book in Canada, plus 25¢ shipping and handling per book and applicable taxes, if any*. That's a savings of about 15% off the cover price! I understand that accepting the 2 free books and gifts places me under no obligation to buy anything. I can always return a shipment and cancel at any time. Even if I never buy another book from Harlequin, the two free books and gifts are mine to keep forever.

153 HDN ELX4 353 HDN ELYG

Name	(PLEASE PRINT)	
Address		Apt.
City	State/Prov.	Zip/Postal Code

Signature (if under 18, a parent or guardian must sign)

Mail to the **Harlequin Reader Service**®:
IN U.S.A.: P.O. Box 1867, Buffalo, NY 14240-1867
IN CANADA: P.O. Box 609, Fort Erie, Ontario L2A 5X3

Not valid to current Harlequin Everlasting Love subscribers.

Want to try two free books from another line?
Call 1-800-873-8635 or visit www.morefreebooks.com.

* Terms and prices subject to change without notice. NY residents add applicable sales tax. Canadian residents will be charged applicable provincial taxes and GST. This offer is limited to one order per household. All orders subject to approval. Credit or debit balances in a customer's account(s) may be offset by any other outstanding balance owed by or to the customer. Please allow 4 to 6 weeks for delivery.

Your Privacy: Harlequin is committed to protecting your privacy. Our Privacy Policy is available online at www.eHarlequin.com or upon request from the Reader Service. From time to time we make our lists of customers available to reputable firms who may have a product or service of interest to you. If you would prefer we not share your name and address, please check here. ☐

HEL07

HARLEQUIN

//// **NASCAR**

In February...

Collect all 4 debut novels in
the Harlequin NASCAR series.

SPEED DATING
by *USA TODAY* bestselling author
Nancy Warren

*On sale
February
2007*

THUNDERSTRUCK
by Roxanne St. Claire

HEARTS UNDER CAUTION
by Gina Wilkins

DANGER ZONE
by Debra Webb

And in May don't miss...

Gabby, a gutsy female NASCAR driver,
can't believe her mother is harping at her
again. How many times does she have
to say it? She's not going to help run the
family's corporation. She's not shopping
for a husband of the right pedigree. And
there's no way she's giving up racing!

SPEED BUMPS is one of four
*exciting Harlequin NASCAR books that
will go on sale in May.*

SEE COUPON INSIDE.

www.GetYourHeartRacing.com   NASCARMAY

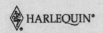